BLOODAXE BOOKS

Shena Mackay

An Advent Calendar

Shena Mackay was born in Edinburgh. She began writing at an early age. Her first novels *Toddler on the Run* and *Dust Falls on Eugene Schlumburger* (published together in 1964) won her immediate attention as a young writer of great talent. *Toddler on the Run* was adapted for television as one of the BBC's Wednesday Plays. Her subsequent novels *Music Upstairs* (1965) and *Old Crow* (1967) added to her growing reputation as a contemporary novelist. *An Advent Calendar*, her extraordinary fifth novel, appeared in 1971.

She has since had short stories and poems published in magazines and anthologies, and broadcast on radio. In 1980 she was a prizewinner in the BBC Radio 3 short story competition. A collection of her stories, *Babies in Rhinestones*, has just appeared from William Heinemann. A new novel is to be published by Heinemann, and another by the Harvester Press. She lives in Surrey with her three daughters.

D1313129

Shena Mackay
An Advent Calendar

BLOODAXE BOOKS

First published by Jonathan Cape Ltd 1971
© Shena Mackay 1971

ISBN: 0 906427 61 4

First paperback edition published 1983 by
Bloodaxe Books Ltd,
P.O. Box 1SN,
Newcastle upon Tyne NE99 1SN.

Bloodaxe Books Ltd acknowledges
the financial assistance of Northern Arts.

Printed in Great Britain by
Unwin Brothers Ltd, Old Woking, Surrey.

To M.M.

Chapter One

An ambulance racketing at four o'clock through fairy-lit Finchley made late shoppers jump back from the kerb as it stopped outside the butcher's shop in North Pole Road. The crew pushed through a small crowd in the doorway to find a white-faced boy sitting on a chair nursing a huge hand wrapped in bloody swabbing cloths, while two butchers crawled frantically through the sawdust.

'It's no use. It must have gone in the mincer like I said,' said one, straightening up.

'He chopped off his finger and we can't find it,' he explained to the ambulance crew who were supporting the stricken boy to his feet.

'Mincer, mincer,' ran through the crowd like a flame.

'Get the mincer,' said an ambulance man.

'Empty,' replied the butcher mournfully.

'What do you mean, empty? Every sec's vital, you know.'

'There was a customer here when it happened, Mick was serving him when the cleaver slipped, so I thought I'd better finish his order for him. I must have accidentally knocked his finger in with the meat. It could have happened to anyone.'

He seemed upset by the intrusion of alien meat and blood and sank on to the chair vacated by Mick.

'You find that finger,' said the ambulance man, jabbing his own menacingly, 'and get it round the Whittington Casualty right away.'

The butcher's pate bubbled with panic. They left, and the butchers heard the siren shrieking all the way down the High Road as they bent their tonsured heads once more into the sawdust.

John put the wet paper of mince on his uncle's kitchen table and went upstairs to see if his cold was any better. Although many wires ended in frayed bunches and broken filaments tinkled in dead bulbs, the house was lit by water, glass and pale growths. A herd of etiolated antlers started from a box of seed potatoes in the hall; veteran eggs crumbled in water-glass, ready to burst like evil puff-balls at a touch; a picture of John's mother had slid behind a tank, and fish swam in and out of her eyes and mouth and shook the interstices of her hat. A dusty glass-eyed fox and two hares were the ignoble trophies that stared from the walls of the hall, their eyes signalling amber through a pall of dust as John went up to Cecil's room.

'How are you feeling now?'

'Weak as water.'

'Oh dear. Well, I've brought something to keep your strength up, which I'll go and cook now. I've got a proposition to put to you afterwards.'

He bared his teeth nervously and withdrew his head. Cecil drew out a copy of *Exchange and Mart* from his army blanket, placed a square of chocolate to marinate on his tongue and awaited the scent of food.

Downstairs, his stomach shaking in memory of the accident but wanting food, John stuck a bunch of spaghetti in one of Cecil's black pots and poured the mince, with herbs, salt and pepper and a tin of tomatoes, into another pot, set it on a low gas and sat down to read the evening paper.

A reeking strip of towel hung from a nail in the bathroom door; Cecil wiped his face on it. He was wearing a bald brown dressing-gown and his bare feet had churned to mud the pool of slopped water under the basin; the bath's iron legs splayed on the floor, pale ships undulated on plastic curtains at the window. He padded out, tying a tie loosely round his robe, huge white head slightly shaking, and then slid one swaying calf after the other down the stairs. He tottered in and poked at the wild white drowned hair of the spaghetti.

'This is done.'

John drained it and poured on the sauce. Cecil was already seated at the table, knife and fork alert.

'Lovely grub,' he said, spooning in a piece of tomato that slipped over his mottled lip. He removed a transparent sliver from his mouth and placed it at the side of his plate.

'Piece of gristle.'

John averted his eyes, tried to force a forkful of food past the apprehension in his throat, felt something hard in his mouth, removed it surreptitiously and pushed away his plate.

'I'll have it,' said Cecil, tipping the contents of the plate on to his own.

'Thought you were as weak as water.'

'Don't want me to stay that way do you?' licking the back of his spoon. 'I have to keep my strength up. Best not overdo it first day up, though.' His straggly white feet crawled into his slippers and thence upstairs.

The front-door bell rang and someone beat on the stained-glass birds.

John opened the door.

'Well, thank the Lord it's you!' said the butcher on the doorstep. 'My mate thought you was heading for here — he's seen you before. Where's that mince you bought just now? Just after the accident.'

'Mince?'

John's heart clenched like a fist.

'Come on mate, let's have it. It's a matter of life and death!'

Had he poisoned Cecil? Would the house be his?

'Why, what was wrong with it?'

'There's only that young kid's finger in there, that's all. So let's have it. I've got to get it round to the hospital right away.'

A transparent sliver of gristle pierced John's throat.

'Finger?' he said, 'What are you on about? I've just given that mince to the dog and there certainly wasn't any finger in it. I hope,' he added with a laugh that hurt his face.

'There must have been. Let's have a look at the dog's plate. They can graft it back if they get it quick enough.'

'Licked as clean as a bone I'm afraid,' said John, repelling the desperate butcher's invasion of the door.

'What you feeding your dog on mince for anyway? That meat's for human consumption only, you know. We're entitled not to serve you if you're buying it for animals. There's people starving, you know.'

'It's no good. There's no finger here. Good night.'

He managed to push the door shut against the butcher but his voice came through the letterbox.

'Funny sort of dog that don't come to the door when a stranger calls!'

John sank on to the bottom stair with his head on his knees, his arm pressing a band of swirling red amoebae across his eyes. Horror began to ooze into his brain. He ran upstairs and found a few drops of disinfectant in a bottle in the bathroom cabinet, filled it with water and shuddering drank it to the bitter dregs. Then he bit off a long worm of toothpaste and ran down to the front door, out and along the road after the distraught butcher, who was hunting hopelessly in the gutter.

'Just a minute,' shouted John. 'If there was anything I could do I would. I saw the accident, but that's all. I never saw the finger once it left his hand.' Panic frothed through his teeth.

The words bounced off the butcher's back. John went in. He threw the tomato tin into the coal-scuttle that stood evacuating rubbish into the fender, it rolled off the top and John took it and the remains of the spaghetti and carried them out to the dustbins.

A lush mulch covered the bases of the dustbins overflowing with soiled straw, nail-clippings, spaghetti, bones, bloody paper, glossy curls, shreds and shards of Cecil. John lifted the lid with averted eyes, and shook the spaghetti bolognese in on top and dropped the tin after and it rolled over and smeared its jagged mouth with the meat, and he went back to the house.

The moon had risen and bleating came from a silvery greenhouse in the garden.

John took half a cabbage and a bowl of water and walked humbly down the icy path to Cecil's goat Pickles. Four years ago the bottom half of Cecil's pyjamas had blown off the line and the goat had been suspected of eating it. Cecil propagated the idea that she was always getting into scrapes; hence the name. The nearest the old goat got to pickles now was maceration in her shed, as she stood year after year hopelessly lactating into the sodden straw.

John sat on the edge of Cecil's lumpy flock mattress and began to roll a little ball of fluff along the army blanket.

'I gave the goat some food.'

'Not too much, I hope—she's not getting much exercise.'

'You mean you haven't let her out for days. The shed was a cesspool and she was starving—her water bowl was frozen over.'

'What could I do? I couldn't leave my bed. My water bowl could have been frozen for all anyone cared.'

'I'm here, aren't I?'

'Yes, and I wonder why. You said you wanted to ask me a favour?'

'I said I wanted to put a proposition to you.'

'Synonymous in your case I'm afraid. Dissolve two Disprins for me, please.'

The Milk-of-Magnesia-coated spoon rattled in the cloudy glass. John wanted to ram it into Cecil's snout, but handed it to him.

'I'll be going then, if there's nothing more you want.'

'Just a minute, John. You know I'd like to help you, whatever it is. Not money I hope?'

'Worse.'

'A girl?'

'What would I want with girls? We've got to get out of our flat tonight and we've nowhere to go.'

'Of course you've got somewhere to go.'

'But we haven't, that's the point.'

'Have you no lonely old uncles who would like nothing better than to have you and Marguerite and the children to stay?'

'Oh ... Cecil.'

'There's one very strict condition, though. Do you agree to abide by it? Otherwise I'm afraid you cannot darken my door.'

'I'm in no position to,' muttered John.

'The condition is, that you don't move out of my house until after Christmas at the earliest.'

'Done,' shouted John, clasping Cecil's venous hand. 'I'll see you later tonight—we'll all see you! And thank you. I don't know how to thank you! We'll make it the best Christmas we've ever had!'

He was down at the bus stop looking at a shop window when he saw his reflection smiling, and the word 'cannibal' bounced back at him off the plate glass, removing his smile. He looked farther down the road and saw the butcher's shop was shuttered. He decided to walk to East Finchley Station, fearing that every passer-by was a witness from the shop.

The houses in North Pole Road gradually got meaner until they tailed off into the betting shop, where John had met his agonizing face, with the regulation coloured plastic strip curtain across the door, a locked launderette with a notice on the window saying CLOSED. BOILER EXPLODED and a shop called MOONLIGHT TRADING CO. with a few brass peacocks and toy dead skin animals and corrupting green bracelets in the window, and a mothy sari spreading grey gauzy wings across the grimy glass. A factory stood back from the road, a patch of waste ground used by its employees as a car park, a large welfare centre comprising several clinics, and the last building visible against the white sky before the road bent to the north, a square red-brick building blazing electric light on to the lawns in front where seagulls walked on the glassy grass. Inside, white sparkling pillars rose to a glass ceiling, the entrance was at the back and was flanked on one side by a ceramic sheep deep in daisies and on the other by a red and white cow ruminating over gutters running with blood. Three young mothers swung by their feet from hooks, blood and viscera slopped from their cut throats and were hosed away by a man in white wellingtons. A new arrival came up the ramp and through a gate, looked round uncertainly, a mallet thudded on its skull, throat was cut, skin peeled off to reveal a red and white silk undergarment, edible parts tossed on one pile, hooves and horns clattered to the floor, to end eventually as jellies, like the glossy blackcurrant castle that shivered beneath the spoon at the party at which John's two children Emily and Ivan were guests.

Beyond the abattoir was a council rubbish dump, away from which a dog was limping, his leg cut by a jagged tin similar to the one John had just put in the dustbin.

Cecil had once owned a nursery, but aphids and indolence had undone it, and at the end acres of wasted roses grew down to a stream's dark edge; empty chains dangled from a green-entwined iron arch in the fence, and in a black slime of petals, among slug-trailed panes where long worms and roots writhed through fibre pots, lay a board whose underside heaved with white larvae, and the faint words WOOD'S NURSERY were still discernible. With the proceeds from the sale of his house and land Cecil had bought The Acacias, where he lived on his savings and investments.

Chapter Two

John's key-ring was heavy with redundant keys; he and
Marguerite had moved five times since they were married.
He selected one in the light shining from the hall and
entered the house in darkness; the time switch, pressed
by someone preceding him by two minutes, had expired.
He didn't switch it on again, negotiated the pram and
groped up to the third floor. He poised his key for the
lock, the door flew open and two balloons leapt out at
him.

'Daddy Daddy Daddy!'

It was the familiar nightly cry. He picked them up and
kissed them, the champagne-coloured curls foggy on his
face, their breath sweet with chocolate.

'We've got balloons.'

'Yes. So I see. Lovely. Take your coats off. Where's
Mummy?'

'I'm here.' She came out of the kitchen in her coat.

'I've put the kettle on. You look frozen. Have you had
a very boring day?'

'No.'

He didn't know when her cold lips would be offered
so ungrudgingly again.

'Good. The children must go to bed early, they're
exhausted. Ivan's first party!'

Emily was four and Ivan two.

'Don't put them to bed.'

'Why not?'

'I've got something to tell you.'

'Oh no! Not again! I just can't bear it: I'm not moving again.'

John was unable to cross the room to place his arm round her so he stood with his back to the door watching her hair spread over the draining-board in grief. The children opened the door and he let himself be pushed forward.

'You won't believe me but it's not my fault. Mr Frankl's dead.'

She turned round.

She had never met Mr Frankl, owner of the bookshop on Highgate Hill where John worked, but had once in passing confronted a grey wing of hair and beak over the top of a volume on ornithology.

'How?'

'Heart. Anyway, the shop's closed down. His nephew came this morning and gave me my cards.'

'Oh, I'm very sorry about Mr Frankl. Will you go to the funeral? But it only means you're out of a job. I thought you were going to say we had to move.'

'I've got a job. I went to an agency called Cleaning Boy Ltd this afternoon. I start tomorrow. It's only temporary of course, but what can you expect with half a G.C.E.'

'Oh John, you are good. I'm sorry I was so mean. Was it completely unexpected with Mr Frankl?'

'Completely. Make the tea, would you? I've had a vile day. I witnessed a horrible accident in a butcher's this afternoon as well.'

'In a butcher's? What on earth were you doing in a butcher's?'

'I might as well tell you. We've run into slight arrears here. You know they're coming to look at the water tank tomorrow, well, we'd better be out of here before they come. I phoned Cecil this afternoon but he was ill, so I went over. That's when I saw the accident. A boy chopped his finger off.'

'How much arrears? Why haven't you been paying?'

'I'll tell you later. We'd better get started so it's not too late for the children. Cecil's invited us to stay for Christmas. Isn't that kind? He's really pleased about it.'

'At least this time we've got a little money saved, thank God.' She put her arm round him and the muscle tightened across the back of his neck as she reached past him.

'Here's a letter for you — I think it's our bank statement.'

'Never mind. I'll open it later.' He tried to push it into his pocket, it slipped, her hand shot off his neck and caught it.

'Twelve pounds in the red! Where's all our money gone?'

'There must be some mistake. A computer error … '

'Error! You've eaten it. That's where it's gone!'

'Me?'

'Yes you, with your eleven meals a day, not to mention forty thousand snacks.'

'Don't spoil Cecil's pleasure, please.'

'Cecil's pleasure!'

She swept out of the room to the bathroom, where any tears that might have been falling were swept with the thundering water into the blocked basin and up through the overflow, while a fist banged on the door and silence poured from the tap until the knocking stopped. When she slunk back across the hall she found two suitcases open on the bed.

In two hours the room was cleared; Emily and Ivan were sitting on a suitcase, each clutching a knitted girl mouse, Marguerite was resting back impassively on the dank mattress. John went to phone for a minicab.

'It'll be here in fifteen minutes.'

'What about those?'

She pointed with her foot at a polythene bag of pennies and halfpennies, heavy enough to fell a skull. Neither she nor John liked carrying coppers, so they had amassed on the mantelpiece, in drawers, under the bed, and in an old cider jar.

'We'd better take them. There must be at least two quid there.'

John tried to push the bag into the old baby's bath but it was full of packets and bottles and knives and forks wedged with clothes. All the pillowcases were full, the suitcases locked. He put it down and went to the window. Marguerite slung the bag into the fireplace and threw a newspaper over it. The children cried dismally as she silently and furiously pulled coats on to their limp arms. Six rings at the door. John put his head out into the dark sky.

'It's here.'

He sat with Emily on his knee beside the driver, a broom whispering in his ear. Marguerite, Ivan, and a pillowcase of pots and pans sat in the back. Behind them their rooms, cleaner than they had found them, yellow bedspread stretched over the bed's iron bones, the army boots and paperback of *Gone With the Wind* on top of the wardrobe where John had thrown them on their first day, would glow until the money in the meter expired. Ivan thrashed like a hooked shark on Marguerite's lap. Mrs Georgiou from the room above quit for a minute the sewing-machine where she treadled away her days and nights; her hand smashed through the polythene pane hurling a boot after the car, and they drove off like a grotesque bridal party towards North Pole Road. Knives and forks jumped uncontrollably in the pillow-case, the driver sneered impassively; he switched on his two-way radio and commands from headquarters were shouted through the car. By the time they reached Arch-way Road the children were asleep. In the light of a corner hardware shop John saw a young man carrying a piece of hardboard with a girl pushing a pram as they turned homewards into a side street, and envied them as the car ground on between two giant lorries under the frail iron arch, towards his house of guilt.

Cecil stood with blue and red light streaming from the stained-glass birds above, turning him into a mandrill.

'Well, my dears, I've killed the fatted calf.'

Marguerite knew enough of Cecil's larder – monstrous skinned limbs on plates, a pair of dangling dusty claws rasping in the wind from the zinc grille, a rat's skull – to believe momentarily that he had slaughtered his goat for them, but her fears were allayed when he opened the oven door on a smoky chicken.

'I think I'd better show you where the children can sleep first,' said Cecil, and went upstairs with the children like frightened novices behind his brown robe.

'Why are we sleeping here, Mummy?'

'We're having a little holiday with Uncle Cecil, isn't that nice?'

'I want to go back to our own house.'

Cecil smiled.

'They're tired, I expect.'

Emily and Ivan didn't want anything to eat; Marguerite found tears oozing from her eyes in the cold bathroom when she realized their toothbrushes languished in a mug in Islington.

She had to lie down on the army blanket beside Ivan until they were both asleep and then creep out of the crowded room. As she put a match to the gas to make tea the surface of the stove flared up in a flat spitting flame.

'Some fat got spilled when I was basting the chicken.'

Cecil switched on the television and they watched white northern cars and houses drowning in the first heavy snowfalls of the winter. Cecil put a bottle of sherry and three glasses on the table. Her tired face felt as taut as burnt chicken's skin, she leaned on the dresser and felt a wet circle soak through her sleeve; she lifted her elbow from a saucer of cruddy milk, and said,

'If you'll excuse me, Cecil, I think I'll go to bed now. I'm very tired.'

Cecil turned his deaf ear towards the door as it closed.

Marguerite shut the bedroom door behind her and looked around; the big bed, heavy with blankets rising from cold billows of air, plugless electric fire in the fireplace, brown unnatural leaves on the wallpaper, nothing more. She put on John's corduroy trousers, another sweater and socks, got into bed and lay too cold to move between the ancient sheets, thinking that she must lie there for at least thirty-one nights, because it was December 1st, and saw each day open like a dark door in an Advent Calendar.

*

When John came up an hour later, feeling that he and his family had disappointed Cecil with their gloom, he switched on the light and threw a large envelope on the bed.

'I got this for the children today.'

Marguerite sat up and opened it and pulled out a sparkling snowy picture of Father Christmas and angels, the silvery dew and fir trees and reindeer and birds, rabbits, squirrels and parcels and elves, studded with little numbered doors. She pulled the sheet over her face. John caught the sliding calendar and forced open door number one on an angel carrying a Christmas tree and stood it in the dust of the marble mantelpiece.

He woke at seven to immediate knowledge of his cannibalism and found himself alone. He couldn't stay in bed, and went down the passage to the children's room where he stood in his garish pyjamas on their red and green floor. Among rolled carpets lolling like old cigars against the walls, defunct fluorescent tubes, inverted chairs, three chests of drawers, they slept.

He went down to the kitchen and found Marguerite washing dishes.

'Why are you washing up? Has everyone had breakfast and gone back to bed?'

'I'm washing them so that we can use them.'

'Oh.'

He suppressed his anger. Steam rolled round his empty brain; he looked in vain for the kettle on the stove and saw it sinking in the sink with pink froth bubbling from its spout as it went under and an ancient hank of steel wool floated belly upwards on the surface. John refloated, rinsed and filled it, and placed it above a jet of the marshy gas that issued from the clotted black burners of the stove. Vestiges of Cecil's solitary meals littered the enamel surface.

John was handed a mug of punishment tea and a piece of black and yellow toast holed like a piece of Gruyère.

'What's this?'

'I had to cut the blue bits out.'

'Will it be all right for the children?'

'There's nothing else fit to eat in the house.'

'I'll go and get some cereal. Where are all those coppers?'

'Not unpacked yet.'

She gave him her purse and he went out, but his head returned round the door and said:

'Try not to hate me too much. I'll get us out of here as soon as possible. It needn't be too bad if we don't let it.'

'All right.'

Her mind was on the green halfpennies oozing from the slit bag into the soot. Suddenly the sun revealed every surface freckled with fat.

'If there's one role that doesn't appeal to me, it's that of domestic reformer. This house is going to stay as filthy as it is now.'

'No one expects you to reform it. Would you prefer to spend Christmas in a hostel?'

'If husbands were banned.'

He went out, taking some money from the box beside Cecil's telephone.

Marguerite stood with her hands pricked by electric water staring out of the window, thinking about the children. She looked out on to a garden shivering in the December sun; an elder tree frayed by winter and cats' claws grew from the slate, brick and iron rockery, faded rosehips trailed over pears sinking into the black earth, sparrows crouched like rotting roses on the bushes, a wicked waterfall of glass glinted by the fence where emerald privet sprang up from the next door garden, and an elastic knee bandage blew bravely from the line over the goat's slimy glasshouse. John should have been back. She listened in vain for his knock and heard the tiny thud of bare feet on linoleum upstairs. John knocked. She made fresh tea and went upstairs past his ruby and sapphire silhouette to get Emily and Ivan and arrange them in the kitchen before letting him in. He handed her a dozen tulips over the bare table; the iron green blades were cold but the tight red buds were icy. She showed little pleasure and they were confined in a narrow glass vase. He noticed that the whites of her eyes were grey and confused, her hands hesitant and a stream of clear hot water poured from the teapot into his cup. She snatched it back as if he was responsible.

Marguerite brought the children's clothes down and equipped them for life at Cecil's in old jeans and sweaters.

'What can we play with?'

'Can I paint, Mummy?'

'There's no paint in this house.'

'I'll unpack your toys in a minute.'

John opened a cupboard and a cascade of rusty spice tins and bottles containing damp silt and residue fell at his feet.

'We can build with these!'

Marguerite removed a little bottle of diseased capers fluttering like whelks in their brine.

'I'm off to become a Cleaning Boy.'

'Limited.'

'Of course. Goodbye then. Goodbye children. Have a good day.'

Marguerite averted her face from his kiss. As she heard the front door bang she ran after him and called, 'Good Luck'.

His head, bouncing along beside the privet, nodded a grim acknowledgment, and Marguerite was left in the doorway wondering if he would be run over and this be their last unfriendly farewell.

She thought of Mrs Georgiou throwing the boot, and wondered why, because they hadn't been very noisy, thought of the grimed floor where the children played and went to find a broom. She couldn't locate her own, but found an ancient splintery one outside the back door on the wet stone and took it in, upturned it and found a worm enmeshed in its silvery bristles. As she stood, mustering her fingers to grope among the dewy spikes and pluck it out, she realized that unfairly or not she, as the woman of the house, would be solely responsible for its cleanliness.

Chapter Three

The Cleaning Boys seemed to operate from a curved white house on North Hill. John looked again at the piece of paper almost reduced to rag in his pocket and opened the gate and splashed through grey clouds in the broken mosaic path, found the company's card at the side of the door, gave the requisite four rings and was admitted through two oak-and-stained-glass doors and told to follow fat haunches wavering dimly up stairs lit by grey rain spiralling past the landing window and a rosy light bulb in the hall.

On his first assignment John found a mop hardened to volcanic rock with which to wash a vast linoleum floor. Blue was breaking through the grey like a spring sky where he had scrubbed hardest, but pools of dusty water lay around the furniture's legs and the skirting-boards were fringed with filth. He found a bottle of bleach under the sink and scattered it over the floor, rinsed his mop and looked down to find the floor dappled with white dots which had devoured the dirt and sucked the colour from the linoleum beneath. He took the bottle and threw the rest of the bleach gently until the whole floor was streaked, dashed and dotted white, then he took from a Nappy Service parcel a napkin belonging to the owner of the lobster-pot playpen, damped it, draped it round the mop-head and finished the floor. The napkin went into the dustbin and John went into the sitting-room.

It was white; pyramids of white china fruit and vegetables stood on the marble mantelpiece, a goatskin lapped the legs of the white television, a tall white candle in a white smoked-glass stick leaned in a corner, its black wick smudging the wall. Dust greyed every skirting; John kicked on the white ball vacuum cleaner and sent it whooshing into every corner. He felt suddenly happy and recalled the second verse of a hymn by George Herbert — he couldn't understand why Marguerite made such a fuss about the futility of housework; it was very pleasant and rewarding to watch the room bloom slowly in the winter sun.

He remembered another time that he had indulged his taste for hymn-singing under a vacuum cleaner's roar, and had almost reconverted himself when he unknowingly wrenched out the plug and his naked note hung trembling in the air as Marguerite came in with a blast of frost and shot it down with a baleful stare. He dashed a heavy moisture from his eyes and pursued his melancholy way up the treads of the stairs. A button fell from his shirt and was devoured.

'If a woman loves a man, surely she enjoys looking after his clothes?' he had once asked.

'Not necessarily.'

At ten forty-five Cecil felt well enough to totter down in his tightly buttoned brown jacket, with a white silk muffler making such a dingy triangle between his lapels that Marguerite, turning from the sink where she was washing a filthy floor-cloth, with iridescent arms, mistook it for his flesh and gasped.

'Hiccups,' said Cecil. 'You shouldn't gulp your food so. I've noticed the way you can hardly wait to leave the table. There's a tin of bicarb. in the cupboard. Mix a glass for me too — we'll have it together and then we can have a nice chat while we drink it. Your husband cooked me a spaghetti bolognese last night that was so good I'm afraid I over-indulged. Cheers!'

As they sipped their inert white elevenses from thick glasses they wondered what to say to each other but were saved by a prolonged bleat from the greenhouse — Marguerite said she would feed the goat. Cecil had taken Emily and Ivan on his knees and was giving them tiny aerated sips from his glass.

Marguerite took a bowl of scraps from the draining-board where Cecil amassed them and went out, and Cecil, failing to find relief in his own glass, drained hers, slid the children off and leaned his head on his arms while deciding whether to resurrect a kipper from the fridge or fry himself a huge crackling omelette. His radius pressed up on his left eye and its fraternal twin, his eye-balls fused into a giant egg, dissolved in cocoa and wall-paper-patterns of dismal green, brown and beige stripes, cones and spokes flickered across his retinas until his head dropped from his arms on to the table.

Marguerite's back pushed the door open, and the goat's head followed, her open mouth fringed by a wet brown beard, knees knocking.

'I think that goat ought to see a vet.'

'She'll be all right when she thaws out.'

'She won't be. Look at her eyes, they're streaming and her nose feels like a furnace. Have you got a vet's number?'

'No. She's always survived without one.'

'You'd better go down to the post office and look up the Classified Directory then.'

The fringes of Cecil's muffler dribbled a protest through cold tea he had slopped on the table as he wound it round the Adam's apple grumbling in his stubbly throat.

There was only one place for the goat's dishes; they sank in a heap of porridge and socks in the dustbin as the gate clicked after Cecil. The children were building a wooden zoo on the floor, the goat with a slight re-crudescence of trembling in the legs, lay asleep on the pile of coats; Marguerite turned her attention to the pristine *Exchange and Mart* folded at Cecil's place. Its prose and type and smell were so redolent of Cecil and his house that when she lifted her smudged eyes from the tyres and wires and brides and satyrs lurking in the pages, Cecil materialized in the doorway.

'I've found your chap. In the High Road. Name of MacGregor, 444 4884. Would you mind putting a stitch in these for me? The greengrocer gave them to me.'

He threw a grey ball at her, which split into a pair of fingerless gloves flecked with emerald greengrocer's false grass. One thumb was ravelled to the point of extinction.

'They'll need more than a stitch. I'll knit you some new ones.'

'Would you really? It'll make a change to have a woman around to do these little things for me. Tell you what, you go and phone that vet and I'll put the kettle on and make us a nice cup of coffee.'

He blew on his hands twice and filled the kettle.

'Mr MacGregor has been called out. Please leave your name and telephone number, and your inquiry will be dealt with as soon as possible.'

Marguerite snapped down the phone on the expectant silence, heard the clink of spoons on saucers and lifted it again and redialled. The voice incarnate answered and she faltered her message of a sick goat and was told that the vet would be with her in half an hour, after surgery ended.

'He'll be here in half an hour. What colour would you like your gloves? What colour's your overcoat?'

'I think yellow string goes well with anything, don't you?'

'Well, no. I mean you want something warmer, don't you?'

'Green wool then.'

'Right.'

'I'll keep an eye on the kids if you want to pop out and get it now,' said Cecil, inverting the saucer over her cup. 'I haven't actually got an overcoat at the moment, there's a good Jumble on on Saturday. We'll all go.'

Marguerite took her coat and purse and erupted through the door in an explosion of protest from the children, who wanted to go too.

When she returned with a pair of needles and a paper bag of mossy wool balls Cecil's voice protested from the kitchen and the reply was shattered by the closing front door. Marguerite was stopped by a black coat lounging over the end of the banister. She touched a velvet lapel with a gloved finger and the worn pile didn't respond. She had never seen it before, but it sent her back to the looking-glass to burnish her blue lips and ruffle her damp hair before she opened the kitchen door.

'You!'

'You!'

'Well,' Cecil bustled round them, between them. 'Well,

it seems that Mr MacGregor doesn't share your opinion of me as an animal-torturing monster.'

He hastily stuffed a prescription into his inside pocket.

She didn't reply. Cecil grew embarrassed as they stared at each other. He appealed to the goat; 'Well, old girl — I'm not such a monster am I?' She ignored him too.

'Just a dose of tonic and you'll be right as rain.'

The air was heavy with all the things they could not say because of him.

'Well, don't stand there gawping all day, man! Haven't you ever seen a pretty woman before?'

'I think I'd better come back tomorrow,' said Aaron at last.

'Take care of yourself,' he said, stroking the goat's head and looking through her horns at Marguerite.

'I'll look after her.'

'She's very beautiful.'

'Good God, man, haven't you ever seen a goat either?' exploded Cecil. 'I don't think another visit will be necessary, either I or my nephew will telephone you if it is.'

'Goodbye then.'

Aaron backed towards his coat and Cecil and Marguerite followed. His flying sleeve grazed her cheek, he turned up the velvet collar to caress his neck.

'I take it you'll be sending your bill?' Cecil shouted after him. Aaron smiled. Marguerite ran upstairs lest she hear any scathing comment on the vet from Cecil and was stopped by her face in a landing mirror. A welt was rising on her face and beneath it her cheeks were as crimson as poppy petals.

Chapter Four

Assimilated or eliminated? Fixed fast to his flesh? John stared at his own hands, occupied in the work he now found slightly humiliating. They were clenching a grey string cloth under a torpid gush of N.3 water. Central Finchley lay spread around him; the kitchen window showing him a glassy section of brown grass and a pear tree with a swinging wire cylinder of nuts suspended from a branch, and a greenfinch of duller plumage than the illustrations in bird books pecking peanuts through the mesh, while sparrows waited in the upper branches.

He had once seen a man asleep in the underground with an eleventh finger growing at right angles from his sinister little finger, and grafted the boy's finger on to Cecil's hand for he had eaten more of it.

He wiped his hands on his jeans and went to the telephone. Detergents had dried the oils from his skin, the sere pages of the directory chipped his fingers until he found the Whittington Hospital. After a long conversation at cross purposes with a girl in Casualty, he discovered that the boy had been kept in for two days and then discharged. He also learned, most important, that his name was Michael Keen.

'I suppose you couldn't give me his address?'
'No, I'm afraid we're not allowed to.'

'It's very important that I get in touch with him. I may be able to help him.'

'Well, I'm afraid it's against the rules to give a patient's address.'

'Could you just tell me if he's from this district?'

'Why don't you try the phone book?'

'I have—he's not in it. Thank you anyway.'

'East Finchley.' He thought he heard as he put the receiver down.

He went to the A–K directory without much hope and as he did was struck by a savage headache over and around his eyes. Keen, Sharp and Smart. Names he remembered hating passionately at school, and thought everyone else must too, because they presupposed a sly disposition, and wondered how anyone could live under their stigma.

Chapter Five

Elizabeth, John's elder sister, came out of school after afternoon registration on to the wide sweep of arctic asphalt. Cars huddled like lumps of Turkish Delight at the side of the drive but she hurried past them towards the gate in the mesh fence where an icy tennis ball had lodged. She taught music part-time at North Pole Girls' Comprehensive and was returning to her Islington room.

A black head peered out of the cloakroom door, like a hibernating animal sniffing the frost, saw Miss Wood and withdrew.

Elizabeth, outside on the pavement, felt a sinister lightness in her music case, opened it, found a record missing, turned back to fetch it and came face to face with Joy Pickering. Footsteps in the corridor had forced her into the open.

'Off to the dentist, Joy?'

'No, miss. Clinic. My feet.'

'Oh, I see. Is that why you always wear plimsolls?'

'No, miss!'

'Are you coming back this afternoon?'

'No, miss, at least I don't think so. It depends.'

'Then where's your satchel? Why haven't you any homework?'

'I've done it all.'

'Joy, you're not going to the Clinic, are you?' Joy hung her head. 'Where are you going?' Miss Wood's use of the present tense made Joy look up in hope.

'Home, miss. I didn't have a chance to feed my cat this morning. He's been out all day with nothing to eat. I'll come straight back.'

'No you won't. That's the weakest excuse I've ever heard. Go straight back to school and apologize to who-ever's taking you for being so late.'

'It's only games. I'll come straight back.'

'Hurry up, Joy. I can't wait out here in the cold all afternoon.'

Joy flashed a defiant look at the road outside and the council houses stretching silently and icily to freedom, shrugged and turned back to school.

Elizabeth went towards the staff-room pleased with her handling of the situation. She had often thought that the girls did not respect her authority, and to conquer sulky Joy Pickering—whose green uniform skirt was defeated in its egalitarian purpose by the stains eating its poor fibre, and by the long darn stretching from its torn pocket and threatening to expose the goosey thigh beneath—was quite an achievement. She had watched her in assembly that morning during the droning of 'St Patrick's Breastplate'. At the line 'Christ in hearts of all that love me', Joy had stopped miming, resuming at 'Christ in mouth of friend and stranger' but faltering at the word 'mouth'.

The thin hymn-book had slid about in Joy's chilblained fingers, her legs smouldered red and blue above short grey socks—her mother and sister had hidden her tights for a joke—and her heart still heaved from her tearful search and run to the bus stop to see the bus's vile red rear skirting the hill. When the school reached 'Christ in hearts of all that love me', she had closed her mouth lest the staff's massed eyes see, and a teacher chortle in the staff-room: 'Did you see Joy Pickering singing "Christ in hearts of all that love me"? As if anyone could!' And to mention anything as physical as a mouth in their presence was unthinkable.

Now Joy stood among the virtuous coats of her class-mates, pressing the money she had taken earlier from someone's black pocket into her palm, concentrating on the circle of pain that prevented her from doing anything else. The money slipped, Joy sat on the bench under the pegs, saw a magazine and slid it towards her. Her eye fell on a photograph of a dog captioned 'Uncritical Friend'. That was exactly what she wanted. Two tears fell, pucker-ing the picture and she couldn't stop them, her face was bathed in hot water; she held the magazine against her face, rocking back and forwards under a sheltering gaber-dine. She knew her clothes smelled of stale biscuits, she thought she sometimes smelled, she never had a partner, someone would have reported her to the games teacher, she had to walk a mile out of her way every night lest a teacher see her friendless in the throng, she would arrive home to find her mother's cracked yellow heels bulging over the fender, absorbing all the heat from the electric fire, and her sister crunching crisps by the light of the obsolete television. At each item the blackness in her head grew more intense and flooded her chest; her lungs couldn't cope, she was clutching and twisting on some-one's raincoat, gasping and yelping. A tentative hand descended on her, the pin in her mother's old bra flew open, piercing her back.

'Joy, Joy, don't ... '

At these words of comfort on her bleeding back, Joy sobbed more desperately.

'Ssh, Joy, someone will hear you.'

Her shoulders were lifted and she was pulled off the coat and turned, and buried her head in the blessed blouse of Miss Wood.

Elizabeth held the head to silence it. When it was almost quiet she said, 'Do up your coat, Joy, and run home quickly. You needn't come back. If anyone stops you, say you've got my permission. Go!' she added, shoving the wet magazine into Joy's reluctant arms and pushing her towards the door. Behind them the Tannoy boomed, 'Will Joy Pickering please go to the medical room. Will Joy Pickering go to the medical room.'

Elizabeth didn't stop to ask why, they both fled. Outside the gate they walked together in silence; Elizabeth, feeling as if she had failed utterly in her moral duty, asked at length: 'What does your father do, Joy?'

'I don't know. They're divorced.'

'Oh. And your mother?'

'Cleaning.'

'Any brothers and sisters?'

'One sister, worse luck!'

Elizabeth felt she had asked enough. A bit later, three yards from the bus stop, they passed a group of bungalows with gabled triangular windows and Joy ventured to remark that they were really lovely and that she would like to live there.

Elizabeth was touched by the child's sense of beauty, albeit misguided. At the stop she asked, 'Have you got some money for cat food?'

'Yes, thank you,' replied Joy, fingering the stolen two-shilling piece.

'You're sure you're really going home?'

'Yes, miss!'

'Well, goodbye then. I go to the next stop. I'll see you tomorrow.'

'Yes, miss!'

'Joy, I'm sorry that your tour of duty as Library prefect coincided with that spate of book thefts. I for one don't believe that you took them.'

'Thank you, miss!'

'Where did you get that book?' Her younger sister Gay Pickering had come in to find Joy reading the magazine.

'Let's have a look.' She snatched at it with one hand, put the television on with the other.

Her mother came in.

'Mum, she won't let me look at that book.'

Joy held on.

'Look out, you'll break it. Give Gay her book, Joy.'

Joy held on.

'Don't break it,' shouted her mother. 'I want to have a look at it after.'

She grabbed the magazine, pages tore from the staples, she hit Joy round the head with it, and she and Gay each took half and settled down on the bed to look at the pictures.

'Put the kettle on, Joy, you lazy so-and-so.'

Seated, slightly sick, on her own bus, Elizabeth remembered that she was going to see her brother at Cecil's that evening, and decided to arrive early so that she would see the children. When she had heard that he and Marguerite had moved into Cecil's, she had been furious but ashamed. She felt left out and had refused

Cecil's Christmas invitation with the curt reply that she was joining a party of outcasts in the Lake District. When she realized that she must spend Christmas alone or at her parents' café she wished to recant. She decided to take some wine and flowers and sweets with her.

With the idea that the sweets *she* gave them did not harm the children's teeth, she got off the bus and stepped into a sweetshop.

'It's Elizabeth.'

'Aunt Elizabeth to you, young man,' she shouted above the tumult of goat and children round her knees. 'Hasn't your hair grown long,' she cried, entangling her ring in Emily's hair.

The child winced politely. 'Do you wish you had hair like mine?' she asked.

'Stand still, Emily.'

Elizabeth looked round desperately—she didn't want John and Marguerite to know of her blunder.

'Ivan,' she whispered. 'Quick, get some scissors!'

'Ivan's not allowed to have scissors. I'll get them!'

Emily sprang forward and screamed. It brought John and Marguerite out full tilt to the foot of the stairs. They stopped at the sight of Elizabeth, Ivan and Emily intact. Elizabeth's guilty face bobbed like a pale lantern in the gloom—she was hiding a hand behind her. Marguerite noticed immediately the disarray of Emily's hair.

'What's happened?'

'Emily's hair caught on my ring. It's all right now. Do we have to stand here in the dark?'

She brushed her cold cheek across John's cold stubble, and Marguerite dwindled away from the corner of her eye. She suddenly wanted to be alone with her brother without the weariness of conversation with Marguerite and Cecil. She stubbed her toe on the kitchen door, groped in her bag to hide her pain and fished out two packets of sweets, Emily's with a bonus tear *glissando* down the cellophane.

'Well, this is very nice. How's life?' John rubbed his hands together till a blister called a halt.

'Unchanged.'

Elizabeth dared not let her cold feet near the fire lest the incipient chilblain, sleeping lightly in each toe, awake. The children had received their bed-time dose of adrenalin and were rushing and screaming through the house. Elizabeth started covetously after them and Marguerite misinterpreted it as criticism and felt the skin of her face tighten and burn. Cecil entered with Emily and Ivan each hanging from a leg.

'Elizabeth! Come to seek your errant brother? Well, they're all settling in very nicely, thank you, aren't you?'

'Bed-time, children,' said John, eyeing Elizabeth's fat purse, and dismissing it from his mind.

'Shoulders,' shouted Ivan.

'Back,' shouted Emily.

Cecil duly stooped and staggered out, followed by Marguerite, leaving festoons of kisses in the air.

'Still going out with that geography teacher?'

'No.'

'Oh. How's Grubby these days?'

'Gibby? I haven't the foggiest.'

'What's wrong, Elizabeth? You're not usually like this.'

'Oh I don't know. School's getting me down a bit … '

Chapter Six

In the morning John telephoned headquarters and found that he had been delegated to a terraced house near Cherry Tree Wood. He reported for duty and was directed by a tall, gaunt lady, pinning a glazed apricot straw toque over a brown fig of hair, to the inevitable Hoover.

'I'm going out to a Sisterhood meeting. I want this room, the bathroom and the bedrooms done thoroughly. You'll find everything you need in the cupboard under the stairs and under the sink.'

She turned on legs bisected by seams, back to the looking-glass.

John plugged in, flicked a wrong switch, and the old black beast set up a desolate mooing and belched a black cloud of dust and ashes over the little boy stepping over the threshold.

'Get out of the way!' shouted John, as he tripped over the flex.

'Come and get your coat on, Tony, we're in a hurry!' he heard the woman say in the hall. The Hoover retrieved a spoon from under a chair. John picked it up and read 'He careth for Thee' on a blue enamel crest on the handle.

'Look!' The woman was in the doorway, whirling the child round her legs to display his filthy state.

'The Hoover did it.'

'You shouldn't have let him come in. Children's clothes cost money, but I don't suppose you know anything about that!'

'I've got two children.'

'Well, all I can say is I'm sorry for your wife — not that she's any better, I suppose.'

'At least her floors don't look like this. Don't you ever clean it? I thought that who sweeps a room as for Thy laws makes that and the action fine.'

'I have chosen the better part,' she replied stiffly. 'You'd better go. I'm not leaving you alone in the house. I'll inform your agency that I shall not be using it again.'

John held up the spoon to her. 'Tell me,' he said. 'Is this really true? Incredible! And why do you dress like that?'

'It's because, well — because — we feel we can best serve God by wearing seamed stockings and glazed straw toques. Yes! And now are you going to leave quietly?'

There was a heap of sand in Cherry Tree Wood frequented by dogs in the early morning, and on sunny afternoons like this mothers brought their children with buckets and spades. It was on a seat near this sand that John sat, wondering what to do. He felt guilty at being in a park without Emily and Ivan. Eventually he was able to return home, or rather to Cecil's, and thawed his hands in the children's bathwater. Emily would tilt her head backwards in the bath and let the shampoo bubbles be sluiced down her hair, but Ivan screamed until his eyes were redder than the stingless shampoo could have made them. Emily's hair had started as tight buds which had slowly opened and now hung in soft loops and blooms over her back. Ivan had the same astrakhan as John, and strangers often patted Ivan's head to see if their fingers would bounce; a hazard faced by West Indian children too.

Afterwards they stood on the floor, the falling towel togas revealing the tiny girl and boy of bone.

John used to say, 'I like you to drink because it's the only time you talk.' Now he had settled for silence, or silence settled like dust between them.

'He is completely indifferent to me,' Marguerite thought, staring at the television until the screen dissolved like a jelly cube.

'How strange,' thought John, 'that that exotic bird should choose to perch for the duration of its one life on the chair opposite mine. Why does it stay, why not simply fly away?'

Marguerite suddenly longed for a giant gin to bring slushy tears from her eyes to wash away housework's grime.

'Coffee?'

Marguerite raged silently behind the evening paper littered with the day's dead, a blackened brick hulk, victim of an exploding oil stove conspicuous on the back page. Neither of the men had ever gone out to the off-licence during their stay, yet she was stiff with fury at their failure to do so tonight.

The water in the kettle began to hiss and steam. John was encircled by men armed with crossbows, holding back a jeering mob. It was trial by ordeal. If he failed, his family would be killed horribly. 'I must overcome the reflex action,' he told himself and, eyes screwed shut, grasped the handle, a blazing bar of pain, for sixty black burning heartbeats.

43

As he mixed the coffee a sweat broke out on his fore-head – 'If I was in prison I wouldn't know what the children were wearing, what they had for breakfast – nothing. Nothing. Nothing.'

He returned to the sitting-room with the coffee, his resistance welded across his throbbing palm, to find Cecil sitting in the middle of the room with his curls like white slugs round the legs of his chair while Marguerite cut his hair. John sat on the outskirts of their conversation, a discussion of the relative merits of local dry-cleaners, while his hand pulsated in the wet handkerchief he had wrapped round it.

Elizabeth saw the old roadsweeper's cart blocking the pavement transversely a few yards ahead and was about to cross the road, but was barred by swift currents of traffic. A lorry driver shouted to her. She stepped back from the kerb and went on. Thirty-seven starlings flew in the marbled grey-and-white sky, a gull shrieked on an aerial – a wooden arm shot out across her chest. The old roadsweeper chuckled and lowered his broom, leaving a tingling line across the front of her coat.

'You was miles away.' Elizabeth wished she were.

'How are you then? All right?'

'Fine thanks, and you?'

'All the better for seeing you.' Elizabeth smiled guiltily, wishing she hadn't tried to avoid the old boy when a friendly word meant so much to him.

'Oh, well, must dash.'

She changed her bag to the left hand and set her feet in motion.

'See you tomorrow then.'

'Yes. 'Bye.'

She had wanted a serious talk with Joy Pickering before registration, but there wouldn't be time now. She rushed into the staff cloakroom and tripped over the rigid legs of a colleague weeping in the chair.

'Elizabeth! What do you make of this?'

It was Miriam Turle, part-time French and music, grey-maned wife of a poet, holding out a sheet of paper with blue Biro printing.

Finchley C.I.D. H.Q.

Dear Miss Turle,

We are investigating the theft of a consignment of plastic belts from a local warehouse, and have reason to believe that you may be able to help us with our inquiries.

I am dictating this letter to my secretary owing to the Station typewriters being serviced.

CHIEF INSPECTOR, C.I.D.

'What on earth,' began Elizabeth. 'Give it to me – look, it doesn't look very official does it? And what can it possibly mean – plastic belts? It doesn't tell you to report to the police station, does it?'

'No.'

'And there's something a bit fishy about a chief inspector explaining about the typewriters being serviced, isn't there?'

'Yes.'

'Well,' said Elizabeth gently to her friend's bowed grey curlicues of hair, 'I'm afraid it looks as if it's just someone being malicious.'

'But why on earth should I want a consignment of plastic belts? I just don't understand it,' said Miriam, standing up and girding a vast black nylon fur hide about

45

her and buckling the white plastic belt at her waist. 'I mean, I've already got lots of plastic belts.'

'I'd try and forget the whole unpleasant business if I were you. I must fly—I hope to see Joy Pickering before assembly.'

'How odd—I spend all my time hoping not to see Joy Pickering.'

When Elizabeth reached her classroom and breathlessly reached for pens, she found that after all she had to enter a black cross against Joy Pickering's name. She called to her form captain.

'Julie, can I have a word with you please? The rest of you line up for assembly.'

She drew Julie over to the window.

'I see Joy's away again.'

'Is she?'

The bell rang.

'Look, Julie, I don't think Joy's at all happy. She doesn't seem to have any friends among the girls.'

'Well, what can you expect?'

'Part of a form captain's job is to look after the other girls in her form. That's why the girls chose you, Julie.'

'Joy Pickering voted for herself.' Which explained Joy Pickering's single vote.

'Well, never mind that now. Look, Julie, I know you're a kind girl—I want you to make a special effort to make friends with Joy when she comes back, draw her into the life of the form. Things aren't too easy for her at home, you know.'

'Why not?' asked Julie, looking interested at last.

'Well, for one thing she hasn't a father—and I don't think there's much money about. Will you try, Julie?'

'O.K., all right. Oh, I almost forgot! Dinner tickets, Five C,' she shrieked. 'No Frees today – she's away.'

'Here, guess what?'

Elizabeth heard a whisper as she joined the tail of girls filing into the hall.

'Joy Pickering's illegitimate. Miss just told me.'

'Julie!' she hissed.

'Ssshh.'

Miriam drifted past minus a hymn-book, a tissue disintegrating in her belt. A buzz ran through the music staff.

'Concert. Queen Elizabeth Hall, Thursday. Pass it on.'

Elizabeth made a mental note to mention to the careers mistress that Julie seemed better equipped to deal with dinner tickets than people. Joy was taking off her coat in the deserted cloakroom and slipping her fingers into the adjacent raincoat, only to be pierced by a steel comb. A patrolling prefect appeared and Joy joined her classmates in the hall.

'Come and see me at break, Joy.'

Joy was left to trail miserably at the end of the queue, shuffling towards formaldehyde and gristly fish skeletons and grey light seeping through the slats of venetian blinds closed for the screening of a film, 'To Janet a Son'.

'How do you get on with your mother, Joy?'

'I don't really. I mean Gay's her favourite. They're more like sisters really. Sometimes I feel like I'm the mother.'

'How do you mean?'

'Well – I don't know. It's a different sense of humour I suppose.'

'You're the odd one out?'

47

Joy was overcome with desire to bury her head in Elizabeth's plump jumper and cry into the cables, cuddled and cocooned and lost in brown wool.

'Joy?'

Joy realized she had bent one leg behind her and was twisting her ankle in her hand. She dropped her leg.

'I suppose so.'

Voices and blouses swirled round them, the bell sounded the end of break.

'I do feel the odd one out, miss. At home and school. I'm so lonely—there's nobody,' gabbled Joy, laying all her shame before Elizabeth, before she could escape.

'Well, Joy,' said the other biped, laying a stiff forelimb on her shoulder. 'We all feel like that at times, but there's no need to. I've been wondering if you would be interested in earning yourself a little pocket money?'

'Money?'

'Yes. Mrs Turle asked me if I could recommend any-one to do some babysitting for her and I thought of you. Would you like to?'

'Oh yes, I would.'

'Do you know anything about children?'

'Oh yes. I'd like to be a children's nurse when I leave school.'

'Marvellous. I'll tell Mrs Turle then, and you can discuss it with her. Run along quickly now, Joy, or you'll be late for the next lesson. Oh! You'll have to get your mother's permission, of course.'

'I'll write her a note tonight.'

'Write her a note?'

'We're not speaking to each other.'

'I see. Well. I'll come round and see her this evening. Will she be in?'

'She's always in. Except when she goes out,' she added.

Joy was minus a timetable and the gamboge doors and staircases were as indistinguishable to her as on the day she had entered the school. She made her way to the lavatories for the duration.

'Miss Wood—Mrs Harper brought this letter up for you,' said a teacher when Elizabeth went into the staff-room. Mrs Harper was the secretary.

'How funny, thank you.'

Elizabeth took the manila envelope and read her own name and that of the school in red capitals. She roused the seated staff with a gasp.

'What is it?'

'Not bad news?'

'What's up?'

'Nothing, nothing.' She fled into the washroom with the awful words contaminating her handbag.

Dear Miss Wood,

You don't know me but you can expect a visit from me soon.

THE BEAST OF FINCHLEY

So it had come.

She stared into the cracked basin's arachnoid zinc plug hole—he could not know where she lived, or why would he have written to the school? Someone within the building—the caretaker working in his coke hole? Nutty Mr Cobb puzzling over the children's page of the *Hornsey Journal* in the staff-room? Eric Turle? Nobody knew of her terrible fear of the dark. Only yesterday she had concealed it so well when the girls were discussing a horror film ...

*

49

Elizabeth arrived at number sixty-six and found it did not exist. She was confronted and confounded by the garish façade of a launderette; in the yellow light black figures moved around the bulbous-bellied blue machines. Elizabeth walked back a few yards to check the numbers, and crossed the road to see if sixty-six had got mixed up with the odd numbers and recrossed to find herself back at the launderette.

She pushed the heavy glass door and entered the heat; a fine drift of detergent made her sneeze. As the door swung behind her it trapped the peg leg of an old lady's basket on wheels, and precipitated her clean washing on to the pavement. Elizabeth strode through the centre aisle unaware of the clamour behind her, and between the last throbbing machine and the row of dryers on the back wall, located an almost invisible door without knob or keyhole. She pushed it, and it swung open on to blackness which slowly dissolved into a dark staircase littered with skeletal white baskets and unclaimed clothes, lit by a spiral of light from an ill-fitting door at the top.

Elizabeth stood and wondered if she had met her doom; the door closed behind her, the machines pounded like jungle drums. She went upstairs and knocked on the door. Television laughter answered her. She knocked again. The television was silenced. Whispering filled her head, voices panicking behind the door. She knocked again and quavered, 'Joy?'

The door was opened.

'Who wants her?' said a face.

'I'm Miss Wood from her school.'

The grey features, crowded at the front of a small skull, pursed, the head turned back into the room. 'Joy!'

Joy's round face appeared above her mother's head. 'Oh, hallo, miss,' she said, and stared.

Elizabeth surveyed them both and realized that one had emerged from the other. 'Do you think I could come in for a minute?'

The Pickerings stepped back. Elizabeth stepped into a barrage of heat and Gay Pickering's baleful stare from beside the extinguished television. Plimsolls had worn the floor-covering paper thin, and heat seeped through the floorboards that shuddered with the vibration of fifteen washing-machines.

Joy was dumbly shaking a Formica-seated chair at her. Elizabeth sat on it and found the venomous rays of an electric fire directed at her shins. There was a pile of True Romance comics on the table — the top one featuring a girl in twin-set and pearls, her lower limbs encased in a tartan rug while her wheelchair rolled towards the edge of a cliff. A mattress was piled with clean and dirty garments. Gay and Mother slept at one end and Mrs Pickering's scaly feet were Joy's companions on her pillow.

A sink in a mottled damp-daubed recess, a small food cupboard, gas stove and nothing more, except the clutch of library books growing strange damp bluish-white flowers under the mattress.

'Would you like a cup of tea?' said Mrs Pickering, taking the tea-pot from the table and sousing the cold tea-bags within with hot water from the tap.

'No thank you — I can't stay really. I came to ask you if it would be all right for Joy to earn herself a little pocket money by babysitting.'

'How much?'

'Oh, I don't know really, it's for a friend of mine —

another teacher at school – it would only be a couple of nights a week at most. It's all open and above-board. She'll be quite all right I assure you.'

'Oh I wouldn't worry about anything happening to her,' said Mrs Pickering, with a lewd look at her daughter.

'Will it be all right then?'

'I suppose so. I've never been able to do anything with her. How much does your friend pay? I could certainly do with it.'

'I'll find out and let you know. Will it be all right for her to start tomorrow?'

Mrs Pickering's reply was drowned in a blaze of laughter from the television. Gay had grown bored and switched it on.

'Good. I'll pick you up here about seven, Joy. Good night Mrs Pickering. Gay.'

Joy, stumbling into the Turles's lit sitting-room, thought at first that Miriam must be in the same line of business as her mother: when a heap of clothes was cleared off a chair for her and she was sitting with un-misted glasses surveying the room, she realized that Miriam Turle had just returned from the launderette and was embarking on a bout of ironing.

Eric Turle thought it would please a schoolgirl to be offered a drink, and he was not wrong: his words were effervescence in her head before the wine bruised her mouth. It recalled the taste of mashed potato from lunch-time; she couldn't speak but sat swirling the wine into a thick red cone in her glass while Elizabeth and the Turles talked. In junior school she had been an unashamed receiver, receiving on to her plate and devouring un-wanted slops and scraps of food from other children's plates, but now pride forbade even second helpings. She had eaten nothing since lunch.

'Cigarette?'

Joy looked round, saw no ashtray within striking distance and squeaked a refusal.

Miriam Turle was hauling up a huge iron from behind Joy's chair; it swung like a dead rat from its flex. Joy was praying that Elizabeth had not told the Turles that she was an outcast, and wondering whether to act tough so that they would think it was of her own volition, when the iron plug swung fiendishly round and shattered the glass in her hand. Miriam shrieked and dropped the iron. Eric leaped, Elizabeth gasped, and Joy stood in a crimson nightmare while they dabbed at the dirty skirt that hung about her rigid legs and blood dripped on to her shoe as a triangle of glass pressed into the web between finger and thumb.

Without any inner warning she began to cry. They pretended not to notice. Then she felt a huge tissue crumple softly into her fist and a hairy wrist glide back past her own.

Everyone sat down again; Joy's scrubbed eyes glared at Elizabeth, willing a similar disaster to overtake her, but her calm fingers threaded the glass stem with impunity.

Miriam's voice, after apologies, assumed a businesslike tone.

Joy sensed that they regarded it as a simple accident that could have happened to anyone and not as a manifestation of her degradation.

'We're going to a Literary Society meeting tomorrow. Hope that's not too short notice for you? Eric's on the committee – he's a good committee man. I'm not actually, but he is. Will tomorrow be all right? I mean, I know you young people are always rushing off to discothèques and youth clubs nowadays.'

'I'm not doing anything tomorrow.'

'Good. Does seven and sixpence an hour strike you as reasonable?'

'Thank you very much.'

'Shall we say seven o'clock? You can help yourself to coffee and things and the television. I'm afraid it's almost given up the ghost.'

As Miriam's voice went on Joy nodded more vigorously at each point, seized with fear that Mrs Turle had used up more than her quota of words and that Turle would leap up and strike her on the mouth, or at least tell her to shut up. But he sat apparently approving of his wife, and of Joy, in whose room the only uncensored voices came out of the television set, where the most grotesque dances and antics were performed with impunity.

There was a thud on the ceiling; the Turles rushed upstairs. Joy, not wishing to speak to Elizabeth, picked up a white folded handbill that lay face downward on the arm of her chair and read.

East Finchley Literary Society
Thursday, December 6th
Mr Cyril Lush will address a meeting on the in-
vidious effects of the ball-point pen on handwriting.
Members and Friends welcome.

They must be really keen on Literature, thought Joy, to even worry about handwriting.

The Turles returned in single file and Elizabeth said,

'Well, I musn't keep Joy out too long, so I think we'll be going now.'

And Joy, angry at being led away before she could prove to the Turles that she was not as she seemed, half rose and stood bent forward like a scarlet-faced figurehead with her legs pressed against the seat of her chair, while Elizabeth fumbled about for her handbag, found it, took out a tissue, rustled it at her nose, replaced it, buckled the handbag, which to Joy was embarrassingly reminiscent of a tiny satchel, and at last stood up.

'We'll look forward to seeing you tomorrow then, Gay,' said Miriam.

'Joy,' corrected Turle.

'Her sister's Gay,' explained Elizabeth.

'Joy and Gay,' spluttered Turle. 'I don't believe it. Gay and Joy!'

'I fail to see what's so amusing,' said Joy, savagely jerking at the door handle, 'seeing as you don't know either of us.'

'Take no notice of him – he's as nutty as a fruitcake,' said Miriam, leaping up to get Joy's coat, but a snort escaped her as she draped it on the stiff shoulders.

'If your sister's as charming as you, Joy,' began Turle, but Miriam's elbow sank among his ribs and dispersed his words.

'I'll be here at seven tomorrow, Mrs Turle,' said Joy stiffly, and stood burning on the black-and-white mosaic path, while Elizabeth gesticulated behind her, until the door clicked and Elizabeth stood beside her on the path. They walked down the pavement, Joy's head glowing with wine and mashed potato and a fondant tissue caressing her cold fingers.

'Did you like them?'

'Yes.'

'I'm so glad. You mustn't take too much notice of Eric, he's a bit of a tease.'

By referring to it she doubles my humiliation, thought Joy. She sighted her bus stop, felt the vibrations of a bus behind her, but said nothing. The lighted carcase swung past.

'Wasn't that your bus?'

'I think so.'

'You are a funny girl, why didn't you say?'

'Didn't feel like running.'

They stood at the bus stop, Joy's foot in the gutter, her fingers rolling balls of crisp crumbs and fluff in her pockets. She checked a prayer that the bus would come soon, knowing that such a prayer from her would bring about a suspension of service. The wind sharpened, blowing Elizabeth's hair back against the shattered glass of the timetable on the bus stop, carving their two figures out of the blackness of the frost.

Elizabeth couldn't remember how long she had known that she was going to be murdered, but could remember as a child lying stricken in a bath of congealing water, afraid to emerge lest her family had been silently slaughtered with an axe and the killer awaited her.

Now she was lying in another bath, staring at the black frosted window wondering when He might come crashing in upon her.

How can I believe that there is someone whose sole reason for existing is to destroy me? But who says it's his sole reason? I might just be killed in passing. She convinced herself that the anonymous letter was the cruel joke of someone without a sense of humour — John? But the susurration of the shower curtain, time dripping from the tap — her voice had flown and lay fluttering feebly at the tip of her throat.

Nothing happened. No Beast of Finchley materialized.

At last she stood and girded on a towel and stepped out, saw a wisp of ectoplasm swirl up the curtain, turned, and it curled into steam. A towel on the door reached out, drew a wet finger across her neck and subsided slowly, while the bath water drained away like her appointed time. She hung a night-dress on her sodden body and opened the door. Wooden shoulders loomed from doorways and flattened into doors.

What's the point of pretending something might not be when you know it's true? If it wasn't true why would I think about it all the time?

Back in her room Elizabeth took out her writing-case and found that the clasp had rusted. She broke it open and with a stolen school Biro wrote:

Dear Gibby,
    Sorry I haven't written for such ages! Life has been a mad round of parties lately.

There was a long pause while she tried to chew inspiration from the little blue stopper of her Biro, but the only result was a slight laceration of the tip of her tongue, deliciously painful when pressed on the palate.

Her lids were rolling down like unruly railway blinds, and she feared the letter would join the reams of unfinished epistles that blew up from books and shelves and tables to embarrass her, and hastily added:

Are you working at the moment? If not, it would be lovely if you could come and stay for a bit.

Write soon.

Love   Elizabeth.

'P.S. Please excuse scrawl,' she concluded in her neat italic writing, beloved of perpetual schoolgirls.

Chapter Seven

A couplet bubbled through Turle's pillowed brain and burst on his waking lips.

> I must have woken with the pain
> My old wound troubling me again.

What was his old wound?

He went to the window and looked out on frosty slates and speckled ivy. The frost filled him with loathing, he scorched the white granules on the grass but they didn't melt. He let the curtain drop.

Miriam's matutinal shrieks rose from pools of egg and shed pyjamas below. Turle himself was clad in a vest, green-and-white striped trousers, and Empire Made maroon cotton socks that Miriam had got in the market for one and elevenpence. It was seven forty-five on a typical school morning, and he had to dress and breakfast and take the younger children to school. He sometimes washed and shaved, but not this morning as he planned a leisurely purification when alone in the house.

As he pulled a shirt over his head he thought of his many old wounds, none of which could cause him to wake with pain. They were mostly humiliations, changed by time in his mind to proofs of his superiority, and a girl long ago, before duffel-coated Miriam had blossomed in his path on the concrete embankment outside the Festival Hall.

He thought of Joy—there was no pain there—only anticipation.

The inspiration of his cheery whistle was at the sink where the smell of toothpaste was the morning smell of fear. That there was no school today made no difference; her heart was so conditioned by dread that it lurched on holidays and weekdays alike, and unknown Turle held as much horror as familiar school. When his invitation to call in that morning and discuss G.C.E. English had arrived her first instinct was that she must obey without question, then, at the thought of being alone with a poet who would almost certainly offer her a drink, she blushed almost aloud. She knew that all heart-searchings were affectation, and that she would go.

When her mother and Gay had departed with a polythene bag of dusters and sandwiches, Joy returned, through the launderette, upstairs. She drew the curtain across the rusty string, and switched on the electric fire; it threw a painful red bar across her thighs as she knelt before it to remove her skirt and blouse, then a grey slip of her mother's, whose knotted straps left corresponding chafed rosettes on her shoulders, and matching bra, and hid her nakedness beneath a cyclamen quilted housecoat filched by Gay from an unattended basket of washing downstairs. She buttoned it quickly lest she glimpse her contracted flesh and took off the rest of her clothes, and carried them to the sink. A few useless hailstones rattled from the little detergent packet on to the surface of her water and floated without dissolving. She ripped the box open, scoured the sides and rubbed the saturated cardboard strips hopelessly on the grey straps of her bra, but was forced to resort to a balding nail-brush and a flake of pink soap which nestled among tea-leaves in the sink tidy. She de-misted her glasses and looked down – under her reddened knuckles, her mother's slip was putting forth its buds, tiny blue flowers were blooming in the grey foam. The hot tap was exhausted. She plunged her garments into a sinkful of cold water, fished them out, rolled them in a towel and dangled them over the back of a chair in front of the fire.

Below, the driers meted out their heat according to the sixpences fed into them. Joy's two sixpences rubbed worn heads in the crumbs of her coat pocket; they were to purchase two fivepenny bus tickets, and she would have twopence left for the rest of the week. But now she could see no farther than the soaking clothes dripping slower than the clock's ticks on to the floor while she took the nail-brush and applied the same rough treatment to herself.

The wind shrieked round the barren bus stop, a taxi dappled her legs with mud as she waited. Her heart failed as Mr and Mrs Turle's hedge loomed nearer and she sank against a crumbling pillar for sustenance; two white marble lions guarded the gate and she stared up a path of mosaic black and white tiles into the hostile gaze of a marble-haired old lady at a ground floor window, and had to pass on.

Electrocuted by Turle's bell, she was tingling on the edge of the step when the door opened and she was ushered by a chequered silk dressing-gown into the gloomy hall, and followed its folds past a silently accusing convoy of push-chair, tricycle, baby-walker, doll's pram, into the sitting-room. The last time she had seen it it had been mellowed by electric light; now grey light exposed the carpet's threads, a wicker curl dangling from the arm of a chair. The backs of Joy's knees encountered the sofa, and she sat down, fixing her eyes on a vase of fading tulips whose coronets of black stamens scraped the crayoned wall.

'I'm just having a bath. Help yourself to coffee.'

Her breath left her body as Mr Turle left the room. She had relaxed to the point of unbuttoning her coat when his voice floated downstairs. 'Bring me some coffee if you're making it.'

Her first reaction was to run for the front door, but after five minutes' vain beating her head with her knuckles, she crept into the kitchen and was confronted by Mrs Turle's domestic appliances, herbs and bunches of twigs. A willow-pattern clock told her that Mrs Turle's tremulous arms were pleading to a spiritless rendering of 'Marching through Georgia', and she fled back to the sitting-room, her raincoat and a gabardine-green rubber plant. Dust clouded its leaves, she drew a finger along a spine, then she dipped her handkerchief in the dead tulips' water and began to bathe the leaves. She stretched to wipe tenderly the ultimate pale green furled spike, whose newly shed sheath still lay on the earth, and heard a sappy snap beneath her elbow. A lower leaf was cracked. Joy withdrew to her chair. Turle, returning beaded with sweat and soap, his dressing-gown lapels revealing a pennant of crisp hair, saw her sitting upright with a huge watery sphere rolling down each cheek.

'What's the matter? Do you wish you hadn't come? Do you want to go home?'

At this final acerbity, Joy said in a stricken voice, 'Something terrible's happened.'

'Yes?'

'I've cracked a leaf of your rubber plant and now it's bleeding.'

Thick white milk oozed at the edges of two thin wounds. He poked at it with his finger.

'Don't!'

Joy snatched at his hand and pulled it away. He looked down smiling at his hand trapped in hers, and, her face reddening as her knuckles blanched, she realized it, but found her fingers caught. He pulled her to him. His lips skimmed her bowed head and she was glad she had washed her hair, albeit in soap, which had rendered it fluffy and intractable. She was standing on the side of her foot, her leg thickened and pricked, he drew her head up, his lips descended on hers and she rolled her eyes upwards and met the furze of his eyebrows. Patterns swarmed on his dressing-gown, her ankle was swelling over her shoe. After a decent interval she withdrew her face and looked at the rubber plant, waiting in the aftermath of her first kiss. Nothing happened. She dared not look at Mr Turle. He was smiling down at her. At last she cleared her throat and said:

'Where did you get it? The plant, I mean.'

'I think it was a Mother's Day present from the children to Miriam, not me.'

Joy had once seen his children trooping round a supermarket. The oldest girl in an attempt at normality had pulled a headband over her hair, but its elastic showed above her ear, her lacy tights, grey from imprudent washing in Joy's launderette, wrinkled into snow-stained sandals, two boys were knitted from grubby Aran wool, and a tadpole in giant anorak and red tights toddled across Joy's vision before she passed behind a barricade

63

of dented tins, from which Mrs Turle's head rose, bearing a ticket marked 'Reduced'.

'What's happened to the coffee?'

'I forgot, I was looking at your books.'

'Oh well, I'll make it then. Come into the kitchen.'

Steam from the brown glazed cups rose over the beech table.

'You said you were looking at the books. I've got over a thousand, you know. Do you like reading?'

'Oh yes!' she searched for the *mot juste*, which would show Eric that she was a kindred spirit.

'I think a good book is the precious lifeblood of a master spirit.'

Too late she recalled the dim green and gold spines of the row of Everyman Library books in his sitting-room — he would think she had got it from there, not from the school library.

'True.'

Eric read her some of his poems, and waxed so enthusiastic that he dredged out all the old exercise books with his boyish epics and declaimed them in fruity tones while Joy grew hungrier and hungrier.

'How about a spot of lunch?' he suggested at length.

'If you like.'

Joy was introduced to Camembert cheese.

'This is the most delicious thing I've ever tasted,' creamily, dreamily licking her lip.

'You should like it — you've eaten nearly six-bobs-worth.' He added a laugh as the pleasure fell from her face; the round cardboard box remained disquietingly empty. She didn't know yet that from now on each time she tasted Camembert memory would oblige with a snapshot of Eric's mouth.

'I'd better be going soon.'

'I thought you'd be staying longer.'

'No, I'd better get back.'

'You're not afraid of me, are you?'

'Oh, no! I've got to do some studying, that's all.'

Eric thought it better to let her go. 'Of course. Will you come and see me again?'

'I'd like to—if you'd like me to.'

'I'd like you to.'

'I will then; it—it's lovely having someone to talk to.' She fled.

Chapter Eight

'In the summer,' Cecil told the children, 'this garden's a butterflies' paradise. If you want butterflies in your garden you must leave some weeds. Red Admirals and Peacocks like nettles, and Michaelmas Daisies of course — butterflies like purple flowers best. You see those bushes' — pointing at a group of rattling branches. 'They're buddleia — they have long purple flowers and in the summer they're thick with butterflies. I grew them from a couple of twigs I got on a bomb site. You know I told you about that rose garden I used to have? Well, believe it or not there were hardly any butterflies to be seen there, you hardly ever see a butterfly on a rose … '

'Cecil — I'll just slip out to the shops if you don't mind.'

Out in the grey High Road, Marguerite felt disembodied as she was blown along with no steadying pushchair. Sirens shrieked as two fire-engines dashed down the road, traffic standing back at the green light to let them pass. Marguerite shuddered. She had seen blackened upper windows, some of fire's fatalities, faulty oil heaters — a splay-legged monster with twisted metal feet straddled Cecil's fireplace. She had seen his straining hindquarters as he fed it pink paraffin through a blue funnel, as she passed his door. A phone booth stood outside a funeral director's on a corner. Marguerite joined the queue of three outside it, sitting on a little wall. She was going to remind Cecil of his fire and to keep the children away from it. Cold was dissolving her feet, she decided to try her luck in the prefabricated post office opposite. There was a queue at every counter but the kiosk was empty. She folded the doors on herself and dialled Cecil's number in the gloom, and heard his phone ringing above her hammering heart.

Cecil answered the phone – they were still alive, then – and agreed to check his fire. With some reluctance.

She replaced the receiver and was reading the list of exchanges when a woodpecker tapped the glass behind her. Tap, tap. Again. She raised her eyes to the mirror to see this importuner before turning, and stared into Aaron's reflected eyes. The door opened behind her.

'What are you doing here?'

'Collecting my Family Allowance; you?'

'I saw you come in. Who were you ringing? Your lover?'

'Don't be absurd.'

She joined a queue, treading hard on the side of his foot, and if it hurt him half as much as her frozen foot, she was satisfied, because he hadn't telephoned or contacted her.

'You look terrible. Just like a butcher. What have you been doing?'

His eyes were red rimmed, face stubbly, a greasy curl grazed his velvet collar, and white overall sleeves protruded beyond his cuffs.

'I was up all night with a dog and I had to go straight to Surgery.'

'Typical!' Then, aware that she had accidentally

complimented him, said no more and silently pushed her book under the grille to the clerk.

'Have you time for a cup of coffee?'

She looked at the post office clock. 'Just!'

What do I feel now? she asked herself, and found that her palpitations were caused only by the swirling coffee and the hands of the café clock, and thought guiltily of the way her heart used to flutter and thud on the three flights of stairs that led to his tiny room that barely held his bed and books, and the window with its square of stars like a picture on the wall. He had given her a pair of jeans and she put them on and they were neon and the night sky and belonging to the great city and stolen champagne.

'Yes,' she heard herself say. He took her hand between his.

'Thank you. I'll expect you some time tomorrow evening. It doesn't matter how late. I'll be waiting.'

'Why didn't you marry?'

'I only liked one person enough and she married some dreary character from a transport café.'

'Oh.'

Despite her hopes to the contrary, tomorrow evening dawned, and with Cecil and John's active co-operation she found herself on Aaron's doorstep at eight o'clock — ostensibly at Elizabeth's room.

'I got some champagne. I hope you don't mind. It's not shoplifted this time.'

'Oh.' She was annoyed at this deliberate re-creation of the past.

The bottle swam up to its green and gold neck in a little sink of weed and goldfish. There was a cello and a cat and a thick white cotton bedspread trailing down, and blue and gold gas flames roaring. He tested the bottle and found it too warm, and turned to test Marguerite who was cold.

'We're right in front of the window.'

'So?'

'A perfect target for anyone with a gun below.'

'You don't think John would shoot us do you?'

'Oh, I don't know. He's been acting very strangely lately. I don't know what's the matter with him. I think he feels humiliated by living at Cecil's.'

Aaron, fearing his champagne would provoke a maudlin discussion of Marguerite's husband, none the less poured it, after closing the red velvet curtains.

'Remember the polar bear?'

'Yes.' She bit her glass reflectively.

As one of a party of thirty-four in pink and white stripes, she had been condemned, for speaking to a soldier on the train, to stand by the polar bear while others went round the Natural History Museum. A boy began circling and circling the polar bear's case. When the rest of the class returned the odd ball among the candy had rolled. She came back half an hour later with a fleck of ice-cream on her lapel, to find the mistress had spilled the bag and they were rolling back from every corner of the museum to report their failure to find her. It cost Marguerite her prefect's badge.

They met every evening after that and Marguerite failed all her G.C.E.s. Aaron who was studying to be a vet — Marguerite testing him from fading green and violet textbooks in his crepuscular cell — passed with flying colours. Marguerite left school. Her disappointed parents did not protest when she took a room in Hampstead and

69

a job in Foyles, where she met John. They moved to the Isle of Wight soon after.

'Have you missed me?'

'Sometimes.'

'There isn't a street in London that's not associated with you.'

'Oh, I suppose I have missed you.'

'Have another drink.'

'It sounds as if it's raining.'

Rivulets of rain ran across Cecil's ceilings, puckered paper hung in watery sacs, which burst, leaving deflated stars.

'I hope John and Cecil remember to put the bowls out.'

'Bowls?'

'To catch the rain.'

'Forget about John and Cecil. Come here.'

'Easier said than done.' She went.

The effervescence was effective, the room swayed, rain beat.

'Oh well.'

Chapter Nine

Marguerite fell into her own bed and slept solidly for two hours, waking at four o'clock in the snowy morning bitterly bitterly regretting.

She slept fitfully until she forced open her iron eyelids to see John at her bedside with a cup of coffee.

'I've given the kids their cereal. I'm off now.'

When he had gone she looked out of the window to see neighbours returning from the station—trains had been cancelled. John didn't come back, so presumably he had arrived at his destination or his journey had been so important to him that he had floundered on and fallen into a snowdrift.

She dressed and went down. Cecil had made two pink mugs of coffee.

'How lovely. Thank you, Cecil. Ugh! what a venomous brew,' she added when she took a sip. It was made with boiled goat's milk and three spoons of sugar.

'The milk shouldn't have gone off—it's only yesterday's,' said Cecil.

'Haven't you milked her today?'

'I couldn't go down the garden in this, it's over the top of my gumboots. We'll have to hope for a thaw tomorrow. She's got plenty of straw and water.'

Cecil's boots were of ribbed rubber with huge feet,

short legs and khaki toecaps. He took them off and put his feet, in socks knitted by Marguerite, on the fireguard.

'Will you stay with the children for a few minutes, please?'

'Delighted!'

She went into the hall and saw with horror a typed letter propped up on the hall stand, the mirror distorting her name. Had John or Cecil put it there?

She unzipped her boot and placed the letter against her leg and zipped it up again; sadly, because the sight of Aaron's letter made her heart beat faster, but only with fear.

Snow bulged against the back door. She stepped into snow that immediately invaded every seam of her boots. She pulled out the letter and read, 'I love you now and always,' and thrust it deep into the snow, the ink melting as it went.

A single horn stuck through a broken pane as if the glasshouse held a unicorn instead of a goat.

A desperate askew face, with bits of glass and ice in its beard gazed from a frozen bleat. She had butted her horn through the glass and stood trapped with her body across the door.

'Move, Pickles, move,' implored Marguerite, but the goat could not.

She pushed the snow from a mouldering wooden sill that ran round the greenhouse and pulled herself on to it, fingers sliding up the glacier walls, until they grasped a wooden spire and she swung herself astride the roof. Riding this glasshouse in the rocking white field, she changed to side-saddle and bent her ten icicles round the spire and kicked the wall until the exhausted wood and glass sank into the straw below and she dropped down after it. She put her arms round the goat's neck and pulled her head back through the glass, treading on an enamel dish of black ice.

She escorted the swollen goat through the back door into the kitchen where it stood, its stained flanks steaming.

Cecil was obviously shaken by the goat's condition. 'Hallo, old girl,' he said. 'I'm getting so vague I'll forget my own head next,' he added in an appeal for sympathy.

'There's a point where vagueness becomes selfishness,' said Marguerite, regarding with distaste the well-fed ball with its steaming oiled locks on Cecil's shoulders.

The goat pushed her face into his.

'There you are, she wouldn't do that if she was ill-treated, would she?' said Cecil, wincing from her brackish breath. 'Ouch, that tickles, old girl,' he added lamely, trying to conceal blood spurting from a bitten lip.

'Better put some disinfectant on it, her teeth don't look too clean.'

'This is how devotion to a goat pays off,' muttered Cecil, swirling disinfectant into a bowl.

'Stop! That's for the bathroom!'

Too late, the disinfectant was tumbling over his lip and frothing through his teeth. With a roar he plunged his mouth under the cold tap and sluiced it until his jaws were numb. Marguerite handed him a towel. The sun had come out and was making the electric light redundant. Cecil, his hands still wet, approached the switch with his mouth open and flicked the switch with his dripping bottom teeth. A cataract of burning red and blue stars filled his black mouth and he fell.

'A fairly mild shock,' said the doctor. 'But why were you switching the light off with your teeth?'

'My hands were wet.'

The doctor groaned but Cecil groaned louder, tenderly fingering his swollen lip.

When John returned only a round black blister remained of Cecil's encounter with death. Neither of them mentioned the letter. In fact Emily had placed it there. In the excitement they had forgotten to open the calendar and remedied this omission while Cecil brewed the Horlicks.

Marguerite managed to get the next day fairly clean and respectable before it slunk away. She had to bang down the phone on a wrong number which seemed to bring an unnecessary flush to her face.

John stirred before the embers of the television; the picture had been sinking all evening and was now a flickering rim at the edge of the screen.

'Cecil, do you mind if I go out for a bit? Get some fresh air. I can't breathe tonight.'

'No, you go on. I don't mind. I want to see this programme.'

Cecil's old eyes were used to the vagaries of his twelve-inch set in its yellow mottled cabinet; he knew that the picture would return if he waited. John saw green and purple snakes writhing half way round the screen, they swallowed themselves, re-emerged at the tail and slid on. He blinked to clear his eyes and went to the kitchen where Marguerite was giving the goat a dry shampoo; her coat was restored and plumed softly between her horns and on her back, like patches of brown field melting through snow.

'I think I'll call her Doris — she looks kind of Doric.'

'Good name for her.'

John wished she was a dog so that he could take her for a run. Some men he knew would just say, 'I'm going out,' and go. He couldn't. Eventually he mumbled his excuses and left.

He stepped into the stale and sinister air of the almost empty bus and went upstairs, inhaling smoke of cigarettes that he could not afford. He took a seat behind the only two other passengers. It was a few hundred yards before he was attuned to their conversation.

'They're identical twins, you know.'

'They must be very close.'

'Actually they find it very difficult to communicate. Every time Glenda lifts the phone to ring Vanda she finds it engaged because Vanda's trying to get through to her. Their invitations always cross in the post too, so they never see each other. Once they decided on a surprise visit and they each waited for two hours outside the other's house in the pouring rain. They got pneumonia that time. They were cited in a divorce once, you know.'

'Was it proved?'

'No, it was a case of mistaken identity – turned out to be two other people.'

John misjudged his stop and had to walk back to the flats, and up and up the concrete steps. Sometimes the sunset set the windows on fire, or cloudy balconies disengaged and floated in the blue, but now the building loomed like a series of lit cages. John's alien feet brought hidden eyes to the nylon curtains. His heart knocked like his fist on the glass of the door. The door was opened by a collarless man in postman's trousers and socks.

'Yes?'

'Does Mick Keen live here?'

'Who wants to know?'

'I do.'

'And who might you be?'

'I'm a friend of his.'

'You don't look much like one of his mates to me.'

'George! Close the door, there's a draught!'

A little television inside rocked with laughter. Mr Keen lost interest in their dialogue.

'You might find him in the Wimpy. There again you might not,' he said as he closed the door.

John crossed the asphalt past three boys playing football against invisible goalposts painted on a wall. A ball whizzed through the gloaming at John's head, was deflected and landed behind him in a tinkling heap of milk bottles. He ran across the compound with the humiliating thud re-echoing in his swelling ear, and went weeping into Upper Street where rainbow rain fell like hundreds and thousands past lamp-posts and lighted shops, and buses hurtled like thunderbolts from the Angel. The Wimpy's sign sizzled in the black sky.

Its decor was typical of its kind; to John it looked frightening; circles of cropped heads above marbled and mottled Formica, ketchup-coloured chairs, rings of heavy brown boots on the floor. The boys' heads froze like skittles as John stood in front of the heavy glass door. A gibbous hamburger hung from a bandaged hand. Mick's! He started towards it but another thick white paw patted a Coke bottle across the table, a sling swung, a cast shifted. The battery of injuries stopped him. He sidled on to a stool at the counter and ordered a black coffee, and saw the boys reflected in the mirror that ran round the wall, and heard ribald snickers directed at him. In defence, he picked up a copy of a local paper from the adjacent stool, and found inside a letter from Cecil, mourning the demise of the galosh. He looked round, laughing, for someone to show it to, and caught a last baleful belch as his quarry trooped out. He realized that he didn't even know which one was Mick, but decided that his only hope was the bandaged hand; so he kept a few yards of dark freezing rain between himself and the boys; two broke off up a side street, then putative Mick and one companion turned left up a narrow road, through iron gates into the maze of flats. They seemed reluctant to part—they backed away, then laughter crackled across the asphalt, they took another step back, shouted arrangements for tomorrow's rendezvous, turned away, shouted corrections to the plan, and so it continued until the space and darkness between them forbade further conversation. John managed to get his foot on the bottom step as Mick scaled the last flight.

'Mick?'

Mick jerked and stood poised for flight.

'Why are you following me?'

'Come down here for a moment and I'll tell you.'

'Tell me from there.'

'It won't take a minute.'

Mick turned to go.

'I may be able to help you.'

'You!' he gave a fierce laugh.

'I was in the shop when you had your accident.'

'Yeah?' Mick licked his lips. 'So what?'

'I wondered if they found it after all, your finger I mean.'

'It wasn't found.'

'Oh.' The darkness filled John's lungs as hope expired; his tongue thickened and groped for words.

'How could you help me then?'

'I think I'd better go.'

'No, hang on. How could you help me?'

'I could give you one of my fingers.'

'What?'

'You heard.'

'What's it to you? Do you know what I think? I think you're a bit of a nutter.'

'Show me your hand. No, the other one.'

John climbed up to Mick and laid his hand alongside Mick's in the light from someone's window. He saw the worth of the gift he was offering. His fingers were an inch longer than Mick's, they lay like bones beside Mick's sleek paw with its neatly buffed nails; Mick's hand rasped on John's rough skin as he withdrew it.

'No thanks.'

John closed his hand on the two little callouses formed by unaccustomed friction of broom handles, Hoover stems and peeling knives.

'Yes, well. It was worth a try, I suppose.' He mustered his rejected flesh and began to descend.

'Look it's no joke losing a finger, you know, it's like losing a part of yourself. Not only that, I've lost my job too.'

Mick's words of comfort fell on the wind.

'How long must I bear this awful mistake?' John asked himself, and the wind and rain and traffic's drone brought back the reply, 'For ever.'

'Were you and your mates in an accident?'

'No, why?'

'You all seem to be injured.'

'A Pakistani got ugly with us.'

'Ugly?'

'Yes, ugly like you are now. Push off. I know your game.'

Fear of his feeble pursuer glinted in Mick's eyes. His boot flashed out and John fell back. Every bang of his back on the concrete step was solace to his soul. Hatred for Mick would replace guilt. He picked himself up and grabbed the boot as it was crashing into his face.

'Do you want to know what happened to your finger? It got minced up by accident and my uncle and I ate it. That's right! I've eaten part of you!' He swung the boot down and banged it on the step; a blue spark flew.

'Oh,' said Mick. 'Oh! I think I'm going to be sick.'

John was not half way up Upper Street before he was leaped upon by Mick, smelling stale, and his friend. He buried his head in his arms, so his body bore the brunt.

Good, he thought with every punch and kick. Good. This episode will soon be over.

John had come back to his uncle, a goat, his wife, and his children in bed. He hung his coat in the hall, put his head round the sitting-room door, was overcome by depression and withdrew it. Marguerite found him in the kitchen, where he stood watching the clean tiles spiralling from his feet. He couldn't speak. He longed for Marguerite to kiss away his bruises and grazes.

'Have you nothing to say after two hours' absence?'

'No. You?'

'No.'

'Tell Cecil I've gone to bed.'

'Tell Cecil I've gone to bed.'

They stared at each other in despair. Cecil's voice came carolling down the hall, its notes snaring them and drawing them back to the sitting-room where Cecil was misdealing a pack of cards.

'Why did I have to get lumbered with you?' she hissed outside the door.

'Who would you have preferred?'

'Oh, I don't know. Someone more like – Paganini.'

He played a progressively stiffer hand and was soon out of the game, and sat, a silent bruise, rigid in his chair.

'Do use the gramophone any time you like,' said Cecil.

'Thanks. I hear the Andrew Sisters have got a good new record out,' she said with a mean laugh, and felt immediately more cheerful.

'Nothing on telly, I suppose.'

Cecil leaped through the *Radio Times* latticed by goat's teeth.

'I'm afraid today's been eaten.'

'It's closed down anyway,' said John.

By mutual consent Marguerite and John pretended to fall asleep as soon as their heads touched the pillow.

John awoke so sore that he had to feign 'flu and stay in bed. He lay there on a pillow of elation because he had settled his score with Mick.

As the grey day decomposed, however, exhilaration seeped away and he was left wondering if he had only received just punishment, and must still make amends.

Chapter Ten

Cecil's tin warbler shrilled seven o'clock into the blackness under her pillow. Marguerite's sleeping feet struck cold lino and she stood in the frost oozing through window cracks dressing herself in the trousers, sweater and socks she had laid out the night before. The kitchen, lit by ghostly gas-fire's light, was satisfyingly smeared with greasy whorls, furniture slouched out of position, garbage stretched the dustbins.

Scouring powder snowed. The mop banged furiously into corners. She turned suddenly. John was in the doorway.

'Have you gone mad? You're wearing yourself out.'

'If I didn't who would?'

'Would it matter?'

Matter! when the legions of dust were waiting to rise up and condemn and choke. A panorama of dirty paintwork assaulted her eyes, they oozed huge tired tears that burned her strained face. She brushed them away and salt burned her dry hands. She found a jar of Brylcreem in the cupboard and anointed the red trembling creatures which were already grasping the mop's handle. John had gone.

When the family rustled across spread newspaper to breakfast Ivan asked, 'Where are our eggs?'

'Your eggs? You children take too much for granted. Well, you're not having any eggs.'

'Don't make the fact that you forgot to buy eggs into a moral issue,' snarled John.

'I'm going to Cecil,' said Emily.

'I suppose you wish Cecil was your Mummy,' shouted Marguerite, and burst into tears.

'Marguerite ... '

'Get to work!'

He went.

Breakfast was completed, the children dressed and work continued. At eleven o'clock she was ready to tackle the bathroom and went upstairs hoping that Cecil had left a condemning rim.

Marguerite turned from the bathroom cabinet mirror in a sudden horrible silence, and screamed at Emily silently splashing gore across the bath from fingers closed over Cecil's discarded razor blade. She managed to hold the blanching fingers under the cold tap's reddening flow and comfort while assessing the wound's width. Emily didn't cry, awed by so real an injury which, numbed by cold water, hadn't really begun to hurt; but Marguerite had to brace her legs against the bath while she washed away the evidence of her child's mortality.

The medicine chest disgorged a roll of sticking plaster and a blue packet of lint. She stuck a piece over the cuts which were long and shallow.

'I'm going to tell Daddy I cut my fingers when he gets home,' Emily said, tremulously.

Ivan came in, glimpsed the scene and began to howl.

'It isn't very deep,' Emily comforted him.

The words meant nothing to him and his cries brought a roar from Cecil's room.

'What the hell's going on? Can't a sick man sleep?'

'Sleep? How dare you sleep while your house is littered with deadly weapons to kill and maim.'

She listened to him shuffling away and bolted the bathroom door, turning on four taps to drown his voice. ' ... my razor – after all I'm not used to children. I'm used to being alone ... '

'You'd better get used to being alone again,' she shouted.

Cecil's head cracked on the door. She knew he was weeping in his awful dressing-gown. Emily and Ivan added their tears to the stream.

'Oh, I can't stand this!' She flung open the door and hurled herself downstairs to the telephone. A woman answered. 'I want to speak to my husband. He's doing your housework.'

A muffled explosion of voices, then John came on.

'Yes?'

'You'd better come home because I can't stand it here any longer and your daughter's cut herself on Cecil's razor.' She crashed back the receiver.

The children had retired to the gloom of their curtained room. She went to hers and rolled from side to side on the bed in an orgy of self-righteous tears, but as they abated and she stared at the ceiling sagging like a badly iced cake, doubts would intrude, and the idea even arose that she had nothing to cry about and had to be nipped in the bud.

Now in guilt and shame she heard the glass door shake. John's voice was shouting in the hall. He was searching downstairs, leaping upstairs. 'Emily? Emily? Emily?'

She wasn't in the bedroom.

'She's washing the paint off her hands,' Ivan told him,

scarcely raising his head from a mess of wet paper and brushes.

'What hospital?' said John not hearing him.

The Elastoplast set sail on the scummy sea in the basin. John lifted out her hand and found the thin white seams across her fingers.

'Daddy, I cut my fingers and it really hurts.'

'I know, my darling. Is this the only hand you cut?'

'Yes and it really bled.'

'I'm sure it did.'

He hugged her to his legs, they overbalanced and swayed against the bath.

'A touching scene.' Marguerite who had come to make peace, and found herself enraged, heard herself say and fled back to the bedroom. She thought of the children as babies lying softly on their pink and blue sheets, and how she could never have imagined herself shouting at them. She rose, determined to salvage something of the day.

'I'm afraid I panicked when Emily cut herself. It was seeing her blood, I suppose. I thought it was worse than it is,' she said stiffly in the bathroom. It was as near as she could get to an apology.

Until now her knowledge of Emily's blood had been restricted to the neat red stitches of a bramble scratch. This was a terrible reminder of flesh's frailty.

'Get your coats on, children, and I'll take you to the park. Let's forget about this horrid morning and have a nice time this afternoon,' she murmured into their furry hoods.

'Haven't you forgotten something?' John was standing behind them.

'What?'

'Lunch.'

'We'll get something out.'

'In Cherry Tree Wood? In December? I take it Cecil's invited too?'

'Damn Cecil,' Marguerite cried, in time for the words to batter Cecil's face as it poked from his door and withdrew like a startled tortoise.

'Now you've done it. I'm going back to work.'

The glass birds shivered on their perches as the door slammed. Marguerite removed the coats and went into the kitchen and started crashing saucepans around, but Cecil didn't respond now to the sound of macaroni rattling in a half empty packet, nor to the children thundering on his door.

The corrugated glass stood blandly in its frame unmoved by John's knocking, his furious breath misted its surface as he stared in at the half cleaned carpet and abandoned vacuum cleaner. His feet, ears, nose and shoulders ached with cold. He thought he would report to headquarters for a fresh assignment, at least it would be warm and he had no money for a meal. He set off to walk. At two o'clock he was at the house on Highgate Hill. 'I'm afraid there was a bit of an upset at the other job.'

'Upset?'

'Yes, I'm afraid so.'

'Like a woman ringing up and insulting your employer and you charging off without a word of apology? That sort of upset?'

'My daughter was — hurt.' He had been going to say 'injured' but superstition forbade. 'Naturally my wife was somewhat distraught.'

'We can't afford to employ people with distraught wives.'

John stared at a Wedgwood cigarette box on the green leather desk top.

'There have been other complaints. Your wife's a bit of a nuisance, isn't she?'

'I wonder if that cigarette box would fit into your mouth?'

'Now, mate, don't get hasty.' Toby backed behind the desk.

'You — you cavalry twill ... !' John turned and went out. On the stairs he felt a sharp pain in his fingers. He looked down and saw the Wedgwood box crumpled like a robin's egg in his hand.

Dense twigs met overhead, ink and saffron suffused the sky, ragged drays drooped in the creaking oaks, and John on a bench in Highgate Woods stared into the trees and thought of nothing. Then his mind went back twenty years and he wondered if the past would give him a reason for his jobless, friendless presence on a freezing bench in a park that was probably locked. A faint bell had rung some time ago and stopped.

Each school-day he left the house, whose walls were lined with sixpenny Penguins and pamphlets and Pelicans, and sheaves and reams of what his parents called Literature, for the new infant school fifteen minutes' walk away. Sometimes he walked with Elizabeth, but her knitted bonnet was usually wagging earnestly in a gaggle of girls and so he walked alone. There was a little girl he had liked very much, but they had had to pretend to hate each other after friends sidled up sniggering at them.

The classroom was a strange, coloured dream. His father had taught him to read from *Forward from Liberalism* before he passed through the infants' gate. Sometimes he poured water from jug to jug or dug in the aluminium sand tray until his nails were green, sometimes he danced to Music and Movement on the wireless, in wellington boots. There was a boy in his class with a clipped ginger moustache but no one he had spoken to subsequently could remember this boy. At Christmas they stuck cotton wool on the windows, and at home they painted non-religious Christmas cards.

Late in the morning (the pale green electric clock's hands were an unsolved mystery to John), evil smells swirled down the path from the asbestos dinner hut, and before the dinner lady called in to check numbers John was paralysed in his little chair while his heedless companions measured lengths of coloured string on blue and yellow shiny paper rulers. John's ruler hadn't worked. His raffia mat was a hideous nest that even the teacher couldn't unravel; its red, blue and green convolutions smudged with tears, the raffia bitter on his tongue.

The bell rang, the children who stayed to dinner were lined up, and those without handkerchiefs sent to blow their noses on lavatory paper, and the children who went home went to the cloakroom. John put his hand in his pocket to check that his dinner money had been stolen. It had. One day the thief had failed to collect and he had bought two bars of chocolate and a cake.

Both his parents worked. His father pedalled away in cycle clips from the house near Wembley Stadium before John was up. He was a meter reader for the Gas Board, and scattered Literature like seeds on his rounds; his mother was a secretary at the Child Welfare Clinic. Later they set up a transport café.

John couldn't eat school dinners. His soft eyes blubbered at butcher's shops, the fleshy fibrous cubes of meat raked from a soggy crust wouldn't pass his throat; those who wouldn't eat sat and sat until they did.

The floor beneath John's chair was littered with chewed lumps of meat and he sat in dread lest patrolling eyes looked down. He couldn't look at the other children eating – he was once sick and allowed to leave the dining-room – but gravy pervaded the potatoes.

Now he didn't go to dinner. He ran to a little recreation ground where he idled among the bottle-green implements, where guilt forbade him to do more than drag a fearful foot from the roundabout, the only boy in the world, fearing to return too early or too late, potential prey of the molester, haunting the road for a returning fed schoolfellow. Back in the playground, drunk on normal air, he played wildly until the whistle blew.

The afternoons weren't so bad; they rested on canvas beds, played on the climbing frame and listened to a story; sometimes John wept, as in the case of a pony who wanted red shoes, two mice whose tree house was blown down, breaking their tea set, and worst of all the terrible shock – like banging an elbow on the table – that Jesus could feel pain and the nails actually hurt his hands and feet. The afternoons sloped pleasantly towards home time, hands together and chairs on tables, but the dinner hour's silence and isolation seeped into his soul and set him apart. Why didn't he tell his parents about the dinners? Or Elizabeth?

The children slept, soft fruits in pink and peach dressing-gowns in their cold room. Marguerite's mood had passed, she stood in the doorway looking at them in the light from the landing, and wished there was some deity she could thank for them.

Silence thundered from Cecil's room. Then she heard him go down to the sitting-room and music flashed and crackled from the gramophone. She forced herself through the hostile air to confront him, but he was lost in the columns of *Exchange and Mart* and she picked out a book from the bookcase and sat down with it. It was called *The Glands Inside Us*, and bore John's father's name in faint pencil. She felt it a suitable penance.

'Very nice, Ludwig,' said Cecil replacing the needle on the record's rim.

'Cecil, I'm terribly sorry about today. This housework mania's got hold of me and I can't do anything about it. It's a disease and I can't cure it. I'm sorry ... I didn't mean all those horrible things I said.'

The great white head swayed to the music. Marguerite thought she would pretend to cry. To her horror she heard herself shout, 'Can't you use an ashtray?' and collapsed in real tears on the sofa.

Cecil came and sat beside her, stroking her hair; a little grey barrel of ash disengaged itself from his cigarette and rolled down her back.

'You and I must have a talk. How do you think the children will remember today? As the day the floors were so clean, or as a day of screaming and tears and banging doors? I think you're getting your priorities wrong, don't you?'

'It's not easy living in someone else's house,' muttered Marguerite. 'The whole house is getting out of control.' She struggled with her hands to indicate the grill's black ashes, rancid burners, goat's dishes, yellow teeth, bath's feet, dull taps, sticky mirrors, dribbles of dry cement caught in cobweb nets in corners, billows of fluff rolling under beds, every cupboard ready to spew its load at a finger's touch, the damp fabric of The Acacias on its half acre of silver mud.

'My dear, this house has been out of control for years, and I'm still here. Now if you want to do something really helpful, will you help me to clean out the fish tanks? I've been putting it off for months and they're really getting a bit unpleasant.'

One of Cecil's scaly friends nibbled his nail. He fed them on Bemax, which he also sprinkled on his own food. Marguerite fished out stinking stalks of weed and Cecil scooped up fish in his hollow hand and laid them in the water of a big mixing bowl on the kitchen floor. Slime was cleaned from the glass, stones washed and gravel sifted, plaster bridges restored to glossy brightness, and the fish who had hung for weeks under their gloomy arches replaced in sparkling water.

'A small dose of Epsom Salts completes the process,' said Cecil, and shook the white crystals over the water from a damp packet, like an old wizard in his white hair and flowing gown.

'Where have you been?'

John was removing his coat in the hall, a mesh of moisture on his curls.

'Working late!'

'Oh good. I was afraid I might have messed up the job. Now perhaps we'll be able to afford some Christmas presents?'

John bolted himself into the bathroom in reply. Marguerite went down the hall, water slapping the sides of the fish tank she carried, and at every fourth step a tidal wave engulfed her waist.

*

Marguerite lay in bed thinking of the long road of days that led to a goat's dripping beard in East Finchley. John put his arm round her and heard behind his back the tiny unmistakeable whirr of her watch being wound.

'What's wrong?'

Blackness.

'Mmmmm?'

'Nothing, I just don't like you very much.'

He rolled away. 'Why not?'

'Well you could try squeaking the occasional endearment.'

John, who had drunk a pint of water before retiring, belched. 'I wasn't born for this you know—marriage to a crude belching lout.'

John put his hand on her shaking shoulders. 'I'm not really all that crude, if you think about it,' he tried to comfort her.

Discussion was alien to them. They lay side by side mummified by loneliness.

John forced his silent jaws apart. 'Let's discuss it. Talk about what's gone wrong.'

Negotiations failed. Talks had broken down and lay in fragments on the kitchen floor. Cecil's breakfast bristled in his eyebrows. A siren's seesaw notes blared through the street.

'I'm Archie the Ambulance sounding my bell
Bandages ready, a stretcher as well,
Out from the hospital straight to the town
Where someone it seems has just been knocked
down.'

shouted the children, quoting from their favourite book.

John's heart banged so, he spilled his coffee. 'Don't buy any meat when you're shopping,' he said.

'Why not?'

'I passed by the abattoir. It gave me the creeps.'

'I won't be able to anyway, I haven't any money.'

The long embarrassment was broken by Cecil tendering two limp but potent notes from his dressing-gown pocket and putting them on the table, and then that cornucopia yielding two Polo mints, one of which turned out to be a corn cap.

Chapter Eleven

Elizabeth plucked her copy of *New Society* from the letter-box and it spat a manila envelope on to the mat. Gibby had lost no time in replying, and her answer, in fat upright letters redolent of exercise books and green knickers, was that she had given up her job in a florist on receipt of Elizabeth's letter, and would arrive later that afternoon and meet Elizabeth at the school gates.

'I won't venture into the precincts,' she wrote. 'Staff-rooms still hold their terrors for me.'

Elizabeth thrust the letter into her dressing-gown pocket with a force that indicated that it was not all she had wished. *New Society* joined a pile of unread predecessors on her window-sill.

Gibby stood in the twilight at the gates dividing a stream of girls in two; a frayed duffel-bag cord bisected her shoulder, a pink hessian bag threatened her feet with its cargo of crushed clothes and purple shoes. Her long frazzled hair was caught back from her anxious face with a piece of Sellotape.

'God!' she cried. 'How can you bear it?'

There was no Divine answer and Elizabeth, hurt at having her way of life criticized so soon, strode silently through sniggering girls to her friend.

93

'You're exactly the same!' exclaimed Gibby.

'You are!' replied Elizabeth, then smitten with pain at not being pleased to see her best friend, added, 'It's great to see you!'

She bent to take Gibby's bag and didn't see the old roadsweeper hooting into frozen hands on the corner and marking her with a watery eye.

They passed a convivial evening reminiscing and toasting marsh mallows at the gas fire, whose grille was soon hung with sticky black stalactites.

After placing a cup of tea by Gibby's tousled sleeping head, sluicing her own tea through aching teeth and arriving at school after assembly had begun, on a belated bus, Elizabeth looked harshly through her gritty eyes on the girl weeping with outstretched arms across her desk. A righteous friend stood at her side.

'Why aren't you two girls in assembly?'

'The Charity Tin's been stolen from Karen's desk.'

It was this girl's task to shake the tin up and down the aisles of desks begging alms for a charity chosen by the girls.

'How much was in it?'

'Only one and fourpence.'

'But that's not the point, miss,' explained her friend.

'You're going to tell me that it's the principle of the thing, aren't you?' said Elizabeth. 'Well, get your things ready, I'll investigate this.'

Won't take much investigating, she heard one of them mutter as the automatic door failed to close behind them.

She found a note on her desk to the effect that Joy Pickering and another girl had still not attended their medicals, and informed them of this as her class trooped back. Joy, who had let rise a vain hope that consistent ignoring of palely duplicated summonses with broken dotted lines for her mother's mark had resulted in the eradication of her name from official records, received this blow in the grey portion of blouse that met her straining waistband and stepped back heavily on a passing ballet shoe. The other girl would have a valid excuse, and exonerated, pass cheerfully into Sister's medicated claws. She had only shame. Rumour flew that the pitch was passed unfit for hockey—five streams of girls were to meet for country dancing in the gym. Calm girls drifted towards the changing rooms and uncertain ones claimed partners. Joy, sickened by the need to seek a girl bereft by her best friend's absence and beg her hand, fled to the cloakroom where, locked in her chosen cell, she settled down for an hour's intensive reading of the *Golden Treasury*.

Crackling of the Tannoy filtered palely through the prisoned air.

'Testing. Testing, 1, 2, 3, 4.' Then. 'Will Joy Pickering please report to the Medical Room.'

'Oh, no!' Her blood pounded a denial, drained heart banged drily, protesting against this affront, but—

'Will Joy Pickering please report to the Medical Room.'

'No.'

Silence flooded over and under the door again. Joy tried frantically to marshal the marching stanzas that only beat her doom, and stayed frozen in the brown angle of the wall until the bell rang for the end of the double period and she could drift dully through the crowds, back to the form room.

The form captain laid aside her nail-file by the dried-up inkwell and peeled open a sandwich, sniffed its filling,

95

closed it and replaced it in a paper bag. 'Miss Mahoney's looking for you,' she said, as her nose poked deeper into the bag.

'I know.'

'How could you know, when you didn't even bother to go to her lesson, and your name was called on the Tannoy? Honestly, I think you must like getting into trouble—I mean, who could prefer the toilets to country dancing?'

Joy knew her lonely sojourns had made her into a dank creature from the drains. She sulked beneath her desk lid, longing for the rejected sandwiches. If only she was thin, everything would be all right, was her fervent belief. She ate very little but the crisps and chocolate she consumed contained such massive doses of calories that her dense flesh never dissolved. Her head ached hollowly, she gnawed a sliver of ruler. Kaleidoscopic plans and excuses shuffled and collapsed; she would as usual do nothing, and let retribution seek her out as surely as a pest killer the errant slug.

It wasn't slow. In the corridor she shrivelled in Miss Mahoney's deadly aerosol.

'Where were you in my lesson?'

Her heart thumped wearily in response, but Miss Mahoney, faced with silence and with electric light radiating from her supercilious glasses, began to shout.

'I was in the Medical Room.'

'How can you stand there and say you were in the Medical Room? I knew you were in school because you trod on my foot in the corridor this morning. I've just come from the Medical Room and Sister says she's been Tannoying for you all morning. here Whave you been?'

'In the cloakroom.'

'The cloakroom! What makes you think that you alone of the fourth year are superior to physical education? Your very posture belies it. Oh, go and explain yourself to your form mistress – I've no more patience with you.'

She marched away on furiously silent feet in Elastoplast-pink ballet shoes secured over the instep by a band of grey elastic.

Joy retreated unscathed up a flight of stairs, stared at the rows of closed mustard doors, searched vainly for a lost timetable and returned to the cloakroom. There it came to her that her one and only life was passing in these squalid tiles and walls. She gazed through reinforced glass at curdled clouds and left the lavatory, her satchel squatting in the corner behind her. The corridor was empty, the wide asphalt bare, the iron gate open. She had left never to return.

The staff-room was ringing with cries of 'Have a nice weekend' as the swinging door swung behind departing staff.

'Doing anything nice this weekend?' Elizabeth asked Miriam Turle over a bag of mint lumps.

'As a matter of fact I am,' chewed Miriam, pleased at being asked. 'I'm taking all the children down to my sister's in Essex. They live in an old water-mill.'

'Super. Isn't Eric going?'

'No. He wants to finish a poem. He's been really sweet, though. He insisted on going to the launderette for me this afternoon so that we could get an early start, wasn't that sweet?'

Elizabeth, thinking of the gloomy pile of discards mounting in her wardrobe, sucked a minty filling from a hollow tooth.

*

Washer Eleven was foaming at the mouth; a prototype of the helpful lady who is to be found in every launderette — shouting 'Your load's unevenly distributed,' across the humiliating buzz of a stopped machine to one; 'I wouldn't put that red in with those whites,' to another; helping fumbling fingers feed coins into the slot; hanging a warning on the broken bleach machine — stepped forward and thrust a sponge into its chute.

Fearful Turle, watching the clock, watching the door, wondering why she hadn't come, if he had got the wrong launderette, had already torn his bone-dry washing from the dryer, a broken button burning his hand, and shoved it back into a washer with half a packet of stolen powder.

'Is this your machine? I say, is this your machine?'

'Joy, I've been waiting for you for hours! Can you babysit for us tonight? It's terribly important.'

Joy, overwhelmed at once by the need to silence his inappropriate voice and pleasure at seeing him, toned, 'Yes, yes,' over a rising tide of breath.

'Can you come at seven? You see, Miriam ... '

'Ssh! Yes, I'll come. Go now. I'll see you later.'

'Shall I ... ?'

'No. Get out. I'll see you at seven. Goodbye.'

In her fear of Gay and Mother and embarrassment at the staring lady at the foaming machine, she almost pushed him out, and ran upstairs, while Miriam's and the children's clothes whirled in an excess of suds.

Upstairs Joy embarked on the two hours of guilt at her rudeness that must pass before she saw him again, and paced the floor and shook the fluorescent strip on the ceiling below, kindling Turle's head to a nest of gold wires as he returned for his washing and cast it once more into the dryer.

On his way home he encountered his daughter in the radiance of a lamp-post and was informed that he needn't bother to come back as he had made them so late that Miriam had decided not to go.

However, she went, and he lay drooping his legs through trails of her Heart of a Rose bubble-bath, while petals of glass and jam slid down the kitchen wall where they had been thrown by Miriam's departing hand. Until Joy, nose still smarting from the nail-brush and, she feared, glowing, was at the door.

'Did I tell you I wanted to be an artist once? I'll find you my old portfolios.'

When Joy went upstairs to the bedroom to look at an early picture of Eric's on the wall, she saw Miriam's open jewel box sparkling with spangles and bangles and broken strings of glass and pearl beads and rhinestone earrings and a heavy gilt bracelet with a single hanging blue cut-glass diamond. Joy put it to her eye and twirled it slowly at the white upper arches of the windows, navy-blue smudge of sky, hazy moon, tryptich eclipsed, sky moon tryptich, twigs moon, swooping tryptich on tryptich of smudged blue and hazy moon.

'What do you think of it?' Eric's voice pealed upstairs.

'It's beautiful!' She dropped it back in the box and went downstairs.

'What do you fancy for supper?'

'I think I'd like an egg omelette,' said Joy, who had spotted some eggs and felt that they were the safest thing to ask for.

Miriam had put various left-overs in little polythene tubs for their delight — cold potato, which they doused in ketchup, and processed peas glued together like green marbles on a frosty road.

'Nectar,' sighed Joy, as she impaled the last square of omelette.

Joy went to the french windows and opened the curtains. 'Oh quick,' she called. 'Look at the moon. Hurry—it's flying past so fast you'll miss it.'

Turle opened the windows and the freezing air coursed through their hair.

'It said there would be a full moon in my diary,' said Joy with satisfaction. She felt Turle's warm fingers on her prickling neck.

'Tired, Joy?'

'Yes. I mean no.' She corrected herself in alarm.

'I think you are.'

Oh God. I might as well have gone for that medical. This is just as bad. Think of something nice—just now the lilac is in—

A sudden agonizing pain in her head.

'Joy?'

'Excuse me Mr Turle—a slight matter of the head-board …' she gasped.

Joy awoke with palpitating heart from a dream of Miss Wood stroking her hair—the hovering smile dissolved, her surroundings reassembled into threatening postures and she was left, in the narrow space between a sweating back and the wall, yearning into the sheets, burning at the thought that those fingers would ever fondle her unlikely hair, and went back to sleep.

Turle woke at seven to the sound of his neighbour sweeping salt on a scattering of snow and an empty space beside him, and went back to sleep. He woke again to find Joy dressed and at his head with a flock of papers in her hand.

'These were on the doorstep, I brought them in.'

'You what! Did anyone see you?' He shot up into the cold air as his pyjama jacket fell back from his bare chest.

'No.'

'But Wilkins was out sweeping, I heard him.'

She stood silent in her aura of cold soap.

'Well it's too late now, I suppose. Come to bed.'

'But it's morning.'

Turle pulled her wrist, her knees bent against the bed and she sat down. Surely she was safe in his sweater with the cuffs so warm on her wrists?

'But it's the morning.' She had dressed in vain. 'But I've got the kettle on—I was going to make you some coffee.'

'It will whistle when it's ready.'

It didn't, as Joy had not put it on.

She looked at his freckled skin, and ran a daring finger along the sweaty bones in his face.

'What are you thinking?'

'I was thinking that I'd like to barricade us in and stay here for ever.'

'Wouldn't it be heaven,' he agreed.

Loved. She had never been so happy. She wished Miss Wood could see her now, and fell asleep.

Water cascaded in the bathroom, wickedness dissolved in white waves of sheet, her wandering hand encountered the wire spiral spine of the notebook Turle kept for midnight inspirations under his pillow, unclipped the Biro from its cover and opened it. The pages were blank. She leaned up on her elbow and began to write.

Turle's soft bathrobe shoved away the notebook, the elbow on which she had leaned had turned to a pincushion. 'What are you writing?'

'Oh, nothing. Why do you keep a notebook under your pillow?'

'Well, a poem's like a baby, you know – if it decides to come at four o'clock in the morning, at four o'clock in the morning it comes.'

'But it's empty.'

'Well, do I have to get breakfast for both of us?' he replied peevishly.

'Oh no!' but lay still, only her eyes rushing towards her embarrassed heap of clothes half under the bed, and back to his face.

'Oh very well,' he said, his good humour restored by this advantage. He turned his back and went to a window, lifted the corner of the curtain and dropped it.

Miriam on the path looked up and waved.

A halo of children's voices round her dread head in the hall, her own voice disengaging itself and soaring up the stairs, Joy's frozen torso in the bed.

Turle rushed down to forestall them with effusive cries that echoed bleakly in the hall, but Miriam, sensing that something was amiss, pushed past him, her sandal gouging his leg, and head in hands he heard her cry.

'Joy Pickering, get up and dress! So this is the poem you had to finish!'

The Turle spawn clustered in a fearful jelly in the doorway, knowing only that their father and this girl had committed an unspeakable crime.

Their father stepped forward, but Miriam was a whirligig in his evil hands, her rucksack whizzed from her shoulder, the buckle nicking his ear. As the blood flowed her rage turned towards Joy.

'Go downstairs,' she told the children. They disappeared. 'What do you mean by coming here behind my back? The rest of the staff were right about you. I shouldn't have let you within a mile of my children, you ... you corrupt ... Well, I assure you it won't happen again. You'd better go.' Her voice softened as Joy stood on her precarious legs, chin puckering. 'Couldn't you not have? Couldn't you have found someone else?'

This injustice pulled a tear over her eyelid's brim, it ran round her nose and dripped on her lip. She turned silently to Turle. Caught in her expectant blink, he fretted at his clotting ear, but vainly, for it yielded only a rusty smudge. 'Truly,' he said. 'Truly, Miriam, it was a poem. I was writing it for your birthday, but I couldn't find a rhyme for Miriam and then Joy called. I did make a start. There's that poem I was writing when you interrupted,' snatching the book. 'Listen then.' Slapping through the book with panicking mind and fingers blue, words flashed by, he turned back and, thankful for whatever schoolgirl drivel would fall from his lips, began to read.

'It is your head that breaks my heart
Watching you in the darkness while you sleep
The night winds blowing round the bed
It is your head that scarcely breaks
The light and darkness of the pillow,
Dreams revolve locked in your head
It is your head that breaks my heart
Lying awake while you sleep and scarcely
Breathing, beside me your head on the pillow
Wreathed like a swan in cow-parsley
Where the white mist rises from the river at
    Richmond.'

'Oh Eric!'
Joy waited for him to confess, to shield her, to declare

his love, but realized he was waiting for her to leave. She turned to flee for ever before a tide of tears engulf her.

'By the way, Joy ... '

She withered on her stalk –

'Why are you home, anyway?' Eric asked Miriam.

'We were flooded.'

They saw a tidemark of Essex mud on her shins.

'By the way, Joy, you live in a launderette, don't you? Although one wouldn't think – I wonder if you'd mind dropping these muddy things in for me. And I think perhaps you'd better take the sheets from the bed, don't you?'

'I assure you it's not necessary,' began Turle.

'Get them please.'

He went.

Joy found herself on the wrong side of the front door holding a thick white polythene bag marked LAUNDRY, containing the Turle family's filthy garments and the shameful sheets. Some hundred yards up the road she dropped the bag in the gutter and some of the clothes fell out, conspicuous among them a voluminous white aertex vest which took wing and flapped into the wintry sky, and came to roost on the crossbar of a lamp-post.

'Where are the children?' asked Turle. 'They're very quiet.'

'They've all retired to bed. We got no sleep last night, let's do the same.' She yawned voraciously. 'Fancy you thinking that about my head, my darling!' she murmured as she put her hand on his and they went upstairs.

Chapter Twelve

'A water-mill in Essex in December? Not my cup of tea at all,' said Gibby, draining the dregs from a mug of tea into her mouth. 'Ouch, I've cut my hand on your damned mug.' She put it down to examine her hand and Elizabeth saw two jagged stumps, and emptiness where the handle had been.

'You wouldn't have cut yourself if you hadn't broken it in the first place.'

'I'm sorry,' said Gibby raising hurt eyes over her sucked hand. 'It's only an old thing anyway, isn't it?'

'Yes. It's only a Queen Elizabeth II Coronation mug dating from 1953.' Her eyes filled as she remembered racing to victory that hot June 2nd sports day, her vest breasting the winning line so fiercely that the tape had scorched her arms, and walking across the grass among handclaps like daisies, with grass stains on her knees, to receive the first prize of a china Coronation mug, and running to show it to her proud parents, catching her plimsoll in a tuft of grass, falling, and lifting the mug unbroken from the ground.

'God, yes, I remember. We all got one in the Juniors, didn't we? And Diana Hamilton broke hers and Miss Evans said it served her right, didn't she?' said Gibby, searching for the anecdote which would re-unite them.

'No!' Elizabeth wondered what else Gibby had managed to destroy while alone in the flat. She saw a pile of books on the bed, an ashtray had moved into their place in the bookcase. Gibby's bald slippers had taken possession of the fireplace. Elizabeth saw the lid of a little porcelain box was askew, the lid was inscribed 'Know thyself' and inside was a mirror. She drifted over to inspect it and found a used pink tissue stuffed inside.

'What are you looking for?' asked Gibby as she began rifling through a drawer.

'My tweezers.'

'I've got a pair I'll lend you.'

'Oh, thanks.'

Gibby grubbed them out of a giant tartan sponge bag. Elizabeth took them and slowly lifted the tissue from her porcelain box, carried it to the gas fire and held it in the tweezers to the flame until it flared. Gibby charged blindly from the room. Elizabeth drowned her guilt in banging the ashtray on the side of her tin waste-paper bin, then put a record on the turntable.

'I ... I ... I ... I' sang the record—mysteriously scratched—a serenade to my unspeakable egotism, thought Elizabeth, who was often provided with such signs and wonders by an obliging universe. Her resolve to rescue Gibby from the bathroom was slightly shaken when the stylus came off in her hand, but she went.

Gibby had attempted suicide. The broken sashcord looped a futile noose round her neck, her feet were on the floor.

'Oh Gibby!' was all Elizabeth could say as she despairingly unwound the cord.

Gibby let herself be propelled to the bedroom and sank into a chair, head in hands, exposing a shameful pink ribbon rubbed on her neck by her temporary noose.

'Shall we go out for a drink?'

Her disconsolate vertebrae shook slowly.

Elizabeth dammed a rising tide of irritation and clasped her writhing fingers tightly as they itched for Gibby's neck.

'Well, shall I go and get some in then?'

The vertebrae stayed inert. Gibby's capacity for cider was notorious. At college she had organized a fund-raising contest to see who could drink most pints of cider standing on his head, and as sole competitor, braced against the common room wall, hair and froth foaming on the floor, treacherous stitches bursting one by one in her jeans, downed five upside-down pints and rolled off with all the honours and four shillings for charity, and spent the next morning cleaning the carpet.

Elizabeth took down her coat and stepped out of the hot gassy air into the clammy hall. The amber off-licence blinked in freezing fog, up the road at the zebra crossing a red cocktail cherry stopped the traffic, a slowing car squawked at Elizabeth, increasing her fury; she flung an impotent mouthful of fog at its blinking tail and banged into a coat which collapsed in the brilliant doorway.

Gibbering with apologies she hauled the old man to his feet and was struck dumb with remorse as the cursing face assumed the shape of the friendly roadsweeper. 'I'm so sorry. I'm so sorry. I'm so sorry,' her sibilant tones silenced him, and recognizing her, he smiled at the happy accident.

'Fancy bumping into you here,' he said. 'I say fancy bumping into you, get it?'

'Yes, I'm terribly sorry.'

'My fault. I was dreaming as usual, thinking about the wife, wondering how she was getting along.'

'Your wife?'

'Yeh. She left me years ago. Took our two youngsters with her and I haven't laid eyes on any of them since. I'd have her back though. You might call me weak, but I'd have her back. Loneliness and pride don't mix. You'll find that out some day.'

With reference to Gibby. How his words smote her heart. 'I'm so sorry,' she said, racing in thought back to her room. 'Have you tried the Salvation Army? They find missing people.'

'What's the use? Who'd want me? No, I'll be on my tod this Christmas as usual. Tell you what though, next time you're baking, save us a mince pie. All right?' He hitched up his lonely shoulders and stepped into the fog.

'Oh you must spend Christmas with me,' cried Elizabeth, clutching his arm. 'Please say yes. I'd love you to.'

'Go on! What would you want with an old has-been like me? No, I'll be all right.'

'Really. I really mean it,' said Elizabeth, ignoring the warning that perhaps she did not.

'About one o'clock all right? Then I'll have time to have a pint or two before I come whilst you get the dinner on. I know where you live. At least I think I do,' he added. 'Is it number thirteen? Yes, I thought it was round about that. Here,' he called as she opened the shop door, and his voice pushed past her and roused the manager dozing at the counter. 'Here, I just want to say you've made an old man very happy. God bless.'

Elizabeth groped for the quart bottle, fuzzy with her unshed tears, and loped home to startle Gibby with a hug that caused her to drop Elizabeth's old autograph book whose pages she was turning listlessly.

Relief poured in twin cataracts down her face.

'Get a couple of glasses, Gib, unless you've broken them all when I was out,' said Elizabeth jovially.

Gibby saw that it was safe to laugh and did so, but said over her shoulder from the cupboard, 'Let's use these striped mugs, shall we? Like we used to at college.'

'Sure, whatever you like,' Elizabeth said, struggling with the stopper. She was unaware that her heavy cut-glass tumbler had lost its twin and in its place in the cupboard was a note that said, simply, 'Sorry.'

'Cheers, and I'm sorry I've been so horrible. Getting near the end of term I suppose and everything seems to be piling up on me at school.'

'Anything in particular?'

'Well, there's a girl in my class who's a bit of a problem, and people on the staff getting horrible anonymous letters. Miriam Turle got one the other day.'

'You haven't had any, have you?'

'Oh no,' she said quickly, redoubling her guilt towards Gibby. 'Some money was stolen too, and the trouble is I think I know who took it. She probably needed it.'

'Poor old Liz, who'd have thought when we were at school that one day you'd be on the other side of the fence!'

Elizabeth suddenly saw Gibby in the bicycle shed twisting a girl's arm behind her back and demanding her lunch.

Eric Turle was watching a film on television about an assortment of people—a Nazi, a Negro, a Tallulah Bankhead—adrift in a lifeboat.

'Hey, that's an idea,' he thought. 'An assorted group of people adrift in a lifeboat!'

He felt the old anticipatory buzz and thought longingly of his notebook at the other side of the room. So were born, and died, many of his creative impulses. They were strongest on Sunday mornings, when he was faced with the disagreeable parade of others' achievements, but by the time he had refolded the last back page, they had dissipated like the bubbles on his coffee.

The telephone rang.

'Why does that blasted phone always ring when I'm working?' he cursed to Miriam's sanctimonious back; she had accumulated another heap of unnecessary ironing to scourge him with, and stood with a pile of exercise books on the other end of the ironing-board and a Biro between her teeth; her sawing elbow betrayed no reaction to his excited squeaks.

It was a fellow poet, a rung above Eric on the ladder, inviting Eric to join a poetry-reading tour of Welsh collieries. Eric, visualizing the rows of simple men in Davey lamps shuffling their boots and wiping a tear from their coaly eyes, accepted. When he sat down again and considered the date of departure, three weeks hence, he realized that he had been asked to replace someone who had dropped out.

'I've been invited to go on a poetry-reading tour of the Welsh collieries.'

'When?'

'In about three weeks. The New Year.'

'You're obviously a replacement for someone else.'

Eric wasn't still being punished for the Joy Pickering affair. He had committed one of his other periodic crimes the previous night. He had gone out to buy cigarettes at seven o'clock and returned at eleven forty-five with a fat linoleum-salesman who sat on Miriam's bed and told her that she was destroying Eric.

'My good man,' she snapped at last, seeing that he was about to roll to the floor and guessing that the combined strength of herself and Eric would be insufficient to drag his beery bulk downstairs, 'Eric's sycophants often accuse me of destroying him. It may interest you to know, but probably won't as I doubt if we'll be seeing you again; Eric's boozing companions tend to vanish; that this house was paid for by my father, and it's my job that feeds the children while Eric goes sponging round the pubs. Don't you think that Eric might possibly be destroying me?'

'It doesn't matter about you. Eric's a genius.'

True to the custom of Eric's guests he was sick in the bathroom. He sat weeping and slopping black coffee while Miriam fried the children's breakfast eggs.

'A very genuine person,' commented Eric after he had left.

'Did you think he was imitation then?'

Eric reached defensively for his notebook and sat down and wrote his name rapidly several times.

Miriam shrieked.

'Who's been at my rubber plant? Who's been breaking its leaves? Who's been grossly over-watering it? The lower leaves are quite yellow; it's only a matter of time before they drop off.'

Eric raised his eyes and saw a space where she had stood and stared at it as an idea formed. He waited for it to dissolve and slip away, but it did not.

Hours later he was still sitting there.

He was toying with the idea of a series of humorous

articles about his wife and children, but somehow they lacked authenticity.

'My nine-year-old daughter came home from school and ... '

He crossed out daughter and substituted son; a poem would obtrude.

He changed the television channel and couldn't get a picture, walked past the clock to ring the time and found that it was ten past twelve. The sitting-room was a lit cell in the dark house. He had not been up to say good night to his children. Miriam had retired and left him supperless. He went to the kitchen and opened a tin of beans, poured them into a saucepan, added milk, boiled them together and gobbled them with a spoon, leaving a black furrowed sediment on the base of the pan and a scorched tip to his tongue. Back at his notebook he wrote.

> There is a garden where frail loonies sit
> In the pale sun,
> Earth's dry skull shows through shaven grass
> Under sparse hair their heads go
> Lolling lolling
> Back to the time
> Before anybody knew they were loonies.

He didn't have a chance to speak to Miriam in the morning as he didn't rise until eleven when he woke in the empty house. When the children were in bed that evening he appeared in the sitting-room with his poem neatly typed, and was furious to find Elizabeth ensconced in his chair, with her boots lying knock-kneed on the floor. He deliberately tripped on one and sent it sprawling. Elizabeth replaced them on offended feet.

'Don't want to miss that bus, eh, Elizabeth? You teachers need your sleep.'

He went out of the room.

'Hasn't Eric got rude lately!' said Elizabeth.

Miriam opened her mouth to retort with a reference to the poetic temperament, couldn't be bothered, and closed it wordlessly as she contemplated the hole in a yellowed Chilprufe vest.

The next day found Eric in his spotted silk tie in the offices of *Eclogue*, a fortnightly magazine, rocking backwards and forwards while the editor read his poem.

'Well, what do you think?'

'I'm not altogether happy with "loonies".'

Eric tried to snatch the paper from his hand. Miriam. Joy. It was too much.

'Hold on, Eric. No, I say, just a minute.'

'I'll take it elsewhere if you don't want it. Give it to me.'

The editor's empurpling face cried desperately, 'No, Eric. "Defectives" fits just as well if you just change the emphasis.'

Turle grabbed the poem and slammed out.

The editor half stood behind his desk, swayed, his hands flew to his chest and clawed at his neck as something burst inside; black and purple eclipsed his brain and his head crashed down, halving an onyx ashtray.

Eric's burst of integrity gave him an appetite. He was soon in Greek Street tearing the claws off a lobster.

Chapter Thirteen

Joy had once won a goldfish at a fair. She brought it home in a polythene bag and made it a home in an empty mincemeat jar, with its little drum of food standing beside it. 'She has to have one pinch a day,' she told her mother.

'Nonsense. That goldfish's going to have three square meals a day like the rest of us. What are you going to call it?'

'How about Chips?' suggested Gay, in a rare flash.

The fish's name was Christabel. Mother and Gay referred to her as Chips for the two days of her life. When she was found floating on the scum of excess food, Joy invested the money she had been saving for a tank in a packet of drawing-pins to put in Gay and Mother's bed, but they trickled from the corner of the box and laid a trail half way home from the shop.

She was thinking of Christabel as she lay with the sheet over her face, praying that Mother and Gay would depart without breaking the silence they had observed since her return.

'If that's the way she wants to carry on, she's only got herself to blame. Dirty little stop-out,' Mrs Pickering had told Gay the night that her daughter failed to return. It hadn't occurred to either of them that she might be lying dead or in hospital.

'Anyone would have to be blind to go out with her,' said Gay, and they had both laughed.

Gay was paying a visit to school that morning; her mother was taking a coat found in the launderette to sell to a friend in Wood Green. Unknown to her the coat's owner, failing to find a manageress to whom to report her loss, had run down to the Station in her blouse sleeves and placed the matter in the hands of the police.

'You dress to complement your personality, Mrs Pickering,' said Joy to herself, watching through the thin fibres of the sheet as her mother buttoned the dark-red fitted coat that fell to her puny calves, and laced her black plimsolls with fresh pieces of pink elastic.

'Millie says she knows of a good job that's going. Might suit her ladyship there. Needn't think she's stopping on at school now after what's happened.'

The door banged behind them. Joy lay still under the sheet. A job. Whatever it was she would take it. Vague mirages of petrol pumps and café tables and sweet counters had been forming and dissolving in her mind over the past few weeks, but now this worry was to pass from her. Transformed from the stained outcast they knew, dressed in new clothes, she would pass the school gate at home-coming time, so that especially Elizabeth and Miriam Turle would see how they had misjudged her.

'Who was that, Elizabeth?'

'Isn't that Joy Pickering?'

'Is it? How pretty she is. Funny I never realized before! Those clothes must have cost a bomb. No wonder Eric found her irresistible. He's still pining you know.'

The letter-box flapped at the bottom of the stairs. Mrs Pickering had apprehended the postman in the launderette and been so surprised to receive a letter herself that she allowed him unmolested to poke a letter addressed to Joy through the door.

Joy was smiling at the thought that her mother had unwittingly helped her. She realized the post had been. She knew what it would be.

Thank God she left before it came, she thought, getting up to retrieve the letter. She didn't want her job jeopardized, and tripped over her mother's hairbrush, whose receding bristles were sufficient to cope with her hair.

Poor Mum. Joy saw her brushing back the grey greasy roll and stepping back from the mirror in satisfaction at the grisly result.

How selfish I've been, she thought tearfully. She must have loved me once, now it's up to me to show her I love her. When I've got my job I'll try to make this a happy home. Give Gay more of a chance than I had to be normal.

She picked up the letter and couldn't believe it was addressed to her, and turned it over and over. The postmark was East Finchley, the day before. The letter she had been expecting had been delayed in the post. Upstairs she opened it and read:

My dear,

When Miriam found the washing in the road, I realized the humiliations I had imposed on you. I'm coming round to see you this afternoon, to try to make amends.

Ever,

E.

Mrs Pickering opened her letter on the bus and read through pebble glasses:

Dear Mum,

It has come to my attention that you were never in fact married to the man you claim was your husband. It could be dangerous for you if this information fell into the wrong hands. You will hear from me again.

A WELL WISHER

She looked wildly round the bus for someone to consult; the aisle was jammed with standing passengers — then she hit on the idea of taking it up the school and showing it to Joy's teacher, both to ask her advice and expose Joy for what she was.

There was nothing in the flat that was not functional except the pile of comics; even the calendar hid a fuzzy growth on the wall. There was no paper, there were no pencils, no books but those in Joy's satchel — Gay made no concessions to the pretence of doing homework, her non-regulation bag was stocked with crisps and comics and lined with discarded sweet wrappers.

However, as it was now, bare of Mother and Gay, limpid pools evaporating on the washed linoleum, Joy thought it looked quite nice, insulated by steam and fragrant coffee from the world of the grey spotted pavement below, with assorted dreary heads going about their dull business.

'You make a mean cup of coffee, Joy,' said Turle, setting down his cup.

'Well, there wasn't much left in the tin,' she retorted with burning cheeks.

Too late, too late, Lana Turner flashed across the television beneath a golden cone of lacquered hair, saying to Bob Hope ' ... and I play a mean piano'.

The morning was ruined. She kept her eyes lowered from the strange man across the table.

He attempted to repair it. 'Nice little place you've got here.'

His words hung, undignified by a reply.

'What's the rent like?'

'I don't know.'

'Has your mother been to the Rent Tribunal about it?'

'No. Why?'

'Well whatever they charge is probably too much.' Too late he realized his thoughts had been revealed. 'What did you do after you left on Sunday?' he asked.

'What could I do? I came home of course. My mother and sister aren't speaking to me.'

'Oh dear!'

'I kept looking in the mirror to see if I looked any different.'

'Why should you?'

'Being your mistress I mean.'

'About that, Joy,' his fingers tightened in his pocket round the money he had brought to buy her silence. Miriam had puffed into the sitting-room yesterday lunch-time armed with Elizabeth's register.

'Look!'

'Look at what?'

Her nail scored a deeper and deeper line under Joy Pickering's date of birth.

'No!'

'Yes!'

'About you being my – er, mistress. I think – and my wife thinks – that it would be best for all concerned if you don't come to the house again.'

'But you love me!'

'Now Joy, if you think, I think you'll remember that I never actually used those words to you.'

'Why can't I see you again? I won't come to the house – you can come here. I know you want to. You must! Don't let her ruin everything.'

'I'm sorry, Joy. We can't meet again. I'm going now. Don't cry. And thanks for everything.' He put an envelope on the table and turned to leave, but Joy's mad hands were on his neck, pulling his collar, grabbing and throttling him, begging him to stay as if her tears and blotched face were any inducement. He broke away and ran out leaving Joy staring at the black fold of his sixteen-and-a-half-inch collar.

She rushed to the window and threw it up on the dark blue sky.

'Mr Turle, Mr Turle.'

He turned and saw his envelope flutter from her hand to the pavement, and ran on.

'It may interest you to know that I've been offered a very good job,' she bawled after him, but he didn't turn again and she laid her head on the splintering sill and cried, while the icy wind took the tears from her eyes and threw them after him.

In the bar of the North Pole Turle burned her from his lips with brandy and wondered if it was safe to retrieve the money or if the north-east wind had blown it away for ever.

Gibby and Elizabeth were steaming up the road.

'What really upsets me is being taken for a sucker. How could she? After all I've tried to do. Honestly, Gibby, I've always stuck up for her in the staff-room and now she's really let me down. She must be really evil. Well, just wait and see what she says when I show her this! Her own mother! You wait in the saloon bar, Gibby. I won't be long. Nobody takes me for a sucker!'

As they rounded the corner Elizabeth was amazed to see Joy Pickering hurl something white from the window after someone who impossibly resembled Eric Turle.

Mrs Pickering's words would keep echoing in time to her footsteps.

'I never really took to her somehow, even as a baby.' How long before eczema and wind and general misery proved her right? Elizabeth hardened her heart against Joy.

'After all, each one must make what he can of his life.'

The owner of the launderette appeared from behind a machine and apprehended Mrs Pickering, who had returned, the coat unsold, in an evil humour, a headache jiggling the blue vein at her temple. He stood beneath a notice which said DO NOT DRY WASH DONE AT HOME — THIS MEAN'S YOU.

Joy, coming upon Gay, Biro in teeth, in the throes of its composition, had asked, 'Why bother? What's it to you?'

Gay had shrugged and added a final curlicue.

The owner had been simmering on the bench for two hours now, yellowed by neon, head revolving; he stepped out and said in a dispirited little voice, 'We'll start with the floor. These blue and white tiles are ... '

'Grey tiles,' corrected Mrs Pickering.

'Condemned out of your own mouth. Thank you. Where are the empty cream and yoghurt cartons I provided for the detergent dispenser? Where's that lid I gave you for an ashtray? The chromium's filthy, the walls are sticky and the customers are conspicuous by their absence. There's no money in the bleach machine, two dryers are out of order, a woman came in just now and found an Elastoplast and four cigarette butts in her wash. She said there's never anyone on duty here and this place is becoming known as a hang-out for derelicts and dope addicts. The other night a certain old roadsweeper was observed taking his ease on the bench. I've got someone very interested in the flat upstairs, you know. A Welsh woman, very clean.'

Mrs Pickering heard half and comprehended less.

'I've got troubles too,' she said, breaking open the rhinestone clasp of her black rubbed suede bag and thrusting the letter at him.

'I don't want to read your letter.' He backed away and pulled open the thick glass door.

'I'm warning you, unless there's a marked improvement here in one week, Christmas or no Christmas, out you go: I'll be back in half an hour.'

'Good riddance to bad rubbish,' said Mrs Pickering. Her rubber toe-cap burst and a toe sprang out and lit the way up the dark stairs to the broom cupboard.

Elizabeth opened her mouth and instead of her intended invective, these words fell out.

'Surely that wasn't Eric Turle?' Two red eyes slewed round to answer her.

A horrible idea crystallized in her mind.

'Oh no!'

Joy's silence answered now.

'I thought I'd heard everything about you today, but this is too much.'

She reeled on her feet. Joy solicitously pulled out a chair. Sinking, Elizabeth said, 'How could you? How could you? How old are you, Joy?'

'Fifteen.'

'Fifteen. Do you realize you could have got Eric Turle into very serious trouble indeed? Answer me, Joy. Didn't you give a thought to his wife? One of your own teachers, why, you're nearer in age to his children than to him. Why, Joy, why?'

A pink ribbed jumper bearing a rosette of Gibby's bolognese sauce, crushed raspberry tweed skirt, pale calves that rubbed together and boots too short for elegance.

'Say something, Joy — as if finding out about the letters wasn't enough. And now this. I can't believe it; I tried to help you and this is how you repay me. Well as far as I'm concerned, you've had your chance. I can't bear to think of it — it's obscene,' she almost cried.

Joy stared at her swaying idol until the pink ribs and tweed blurred like its native heather.

'You may hate me but you don't hate me as much as I hate you, because all the hate in the world is in my heart for you.'

'I've never hated anyone in my life. I'm against it,' retorted Elizabeth. 'Let's leave this distasteful subject — I just don't know what to say. About those letters — leaving aside for the present the cruel vicious ones you wrote to me and Mrs Turle — what on earth made you?'

'Letters?' Joy managed to mouth as her blood evaporated.

'The game's up, Joy. How could you do it to your own mother?'

'She's not my mother.'

'Don't be stupid, Joy, she came to me in a terrible state this morning with that dreadful letter you wrote.'

'What letter, and how do you know it was me who wrote it?'

'Because, Joy, the letter started with the words, "Dear Mum".'

'Oh. Oh.'

'So you see you aren't so clever after all, are you? Such stupidity, such an elementary mistake! You'd never get into the secret service.'

'All right, so I wrote that letter but I didn't write any of the others. In fact I don't even know about them.'

'Joy ... '

'If you repeat that inappropriate monosyllable once more I'll kill you.' Joy picked up a handleless knife from the draining-board.

'I want you to come to the staff-room before assembly tomorrow morning. You will make a clean breast of everything to Mrs Turle including the reason for her husband's visit. I'm sure she'll do her best to forgive you. She's a very good person.'

'I've left school.'

'Don't be ridiculous.'

'I've been offered a job.'

'A job? What sort of job would anyone offer you?'

'That's my business.'

'I take it you'll be wanting a reference for this job?'

'I don't know ... I hadn't thought about it.'

Elizabeth was defeated. Her efforts for nothing. 'If you've really made up your mind I suppose I'd better write you a reference?'

'Would you? Oh, thank you, miss. This job's really important to me.'

'Give me a pen and paper.'

'There aren't any.'

Joy thought of her satchel's resting place and blushed.

Elizabeth took a pen and writing-pad from her bag; as she wrote she spoke.

'Your mother came to see me in great distress. How could you be so heartless? She always fed and clothed you and provided a roof over your head.'

'It wasn't enough.'

'Joy, you know as well as I do that your mother's of very low intelligence — couldn't you have made allowances?'

'Oh am I? Go on, out of it. Hop it. Pushing yourself in where you're not wanted.' She had materialized unnoticed.

'But you came to see me —'

'Hop it.'

'Have I meant nothing to you, Joy?'

She gripped Elizabeth's elbow and pushed her through the open door and down several stairs. She slid to the bottom.

'Now who's of low intelligence?' shrilled Mrs Pickering's voice through the darkness.

Gay, who had loitered at the off-licence and come in crackling with crisps, stepped on her and kicked her aside like a bundle of lost washing.

Blinded by the light in the launderette, Elizabeth felt fingers consolidate the bruise started by Mrs Pickering.

'Last time you were in here you knocked over an old lady's wash.'

Elizabeth escaped through the frost to the North Pole.

'Sorry I was so long,' she gasped to Gibby.

'That's all right: some bloke's been trying to chat me

up.' She jerked a shoulder at a head wreathed in plastic vine leaves in the mirror.

'Eric!'

He turned his eyes, already dimmed by three quick brandies, from the reflection to the reality.

'Elizabeth.'

'Hallo, Eric. I've just come from – up there.'

'So you know.'

'I know, Eric, and I want to say that I don't blame you at all.'

Eric surprised himself by ordering a drink for Elizabeth and Gibby. Gibby begged for a Scotch and a Guinness, and Elizabeth, who felt she must compensate, glowered into her tomato juice.

'I've had a great idea. I'll have a party. You must all come,' he called to everyone in hearing distance at the bar. 'At Turle's place.'

'That should cheer things up a bit.'

Back in the launderette Mrs Pickering, muttering under supervision, mopped the grey floor and had to straighten her aching back to deny all knowledge of a missing coat to a policewoman.

Chapter Fourteen

Cecil was on his knees pouring pink paraffin through a funnel into the stove, Marguerite knitting through a blur of tears which occasionally fell and hung from her needles like raindrops on a fence, and John was sitting twisting his fingers, fighting to hear above voices squabbling in his head, finding it hard to sit still.

'I don't like the look of that goat's eyes,' said Marguerite.

'They are a bit baleful,' agreed Cecil.

'No. I mean – look at them! They're terribly watery and clouded.'

'Probably the cold,' said John. 'Yours are a bit red too.'

'Yes, you have been looking a bit pink round the gills lately,' said Cecil.

'I'm going to phone the vet and make an appointment for Doris.' She stabbed her needles into the wool and stood up.

'At nine o'clock in the evening?'

'There's an answering service.'

The door closed on any reply they might have made; she pictured uncle and nephew's shoulders rising and falling at woman's contrary ways.

'Hallo.'

'What's wrong?'

'Don't be so alarmist.'

She nearly smashed down the telephone and severed her lifeline from The Acacias.

'How lovely to hear your voice.'

'Don't sound so placating.'

The conversation was getting out of hand; she twisted the flex round her hand; silence sizzled through the little holes in the black receiver. Try to start afresh. He succeeded.

'Are you feeling gloomy?'

'A bit.'

'Come and see me. I'll cheer you up.'

'I want you to come and see me.'

'Now?'

'Tomorrow morning. About the goat's eyes.'

'Are they bad?'

'No.'

'All right. I'll be round in the morning. Sleep well.'

'Couldn't you get through?'

'I did in the end. He's coming tomorrow.'

'Good.'

'I don't have to go in until the afternoon,' John said.

The ceiling creaked. He heard the susurrating paper garlands endlessly whispering in the draught from the fire. He looked at Cecil's decanter; remnants of bathsalts, its former tenants, grew like a chemical garden on its bottom and imparted a sweet musty flavour to the whisky. Cecil followed his eyes and got three small tumblers, each with a mossy circle of felt glued to its base, from the sideboard. Marguerite put down her knitting to join in the toast:

'To happiness.'

She held up her work and gazed proudly at it and was seized with a melancholy vision of the cardigan grown old, matted by injudicious washing, buttons hanging like dead marigolds from frayed stalks, and ribbing opening in a doomed triangle.

John's mind was turned back to the room where he used to meet his first love. In memory that room was swirling, sofa and chairs whirling, lights skimming ceiling, floor – his mind never lurched like that now, nor his eyes, brain, organs, fused in a terrible batter. That morning a girl had thrown up almost over his feet at the corner of Sainsbury's, clucking people looped out on the pavement in wide semicircles to avoid her. John had held her parcels while she was sick again. He went on his way with prickling skin, tingling at his goodness for ten yards until self-loathing took back the helm. Cecil was refilling his glass. He drank from it without noticing. 'Oh God,' he thought, 'what have I done? You bring children into the world and if they don't die young they die old, and which is worse? Who knows what may happen to Emily and Ivan's grandchildren, and I'm responsible for it?'

John had to press his cuff surreptitiously to each eye. He had thought he suffered from hay-fever until one day he had come home and found Marguerite dusting with his handkerchief; now she used his socks. He wondered what was going on behind Cecil's closed marble lids and if he was dreaming of roses blighted by unpaid bills and unsigned invoices.

'I was thinking,' he said. 'Why don't you tell me what to do, and I'll give the garden a good going over to-morrow morning. Any pruning, composting, there's plenty of compost about the house –'

Why did I say that, he thought. 'Because I wanted to cheer him up, or to make him think I was unselfish?'

The reason didn't matter, Cecil didn't look up from the paper.

'Finished the Junior Crossword yet?'

'Animal. Four letters.'

'Oryx.'

'Thanks. That's it then.'

Chapter Fifteen

Marguerite stared at the navy-blue futile sky of the new day through the steamed windows, and wiping a clean space with the tea towel, saw a misty Christmas postman with his billowy sack come out of the abattoir's gates. She was wearing an aubergine velvet dress, pewter tights and gunmetal shoes, her hair fell in metal chains and loops on her shoulders. John's maroon roll-neck sweater, one of Cecil's jumble bargains, bagged over tweed trousers that hung in a false seat from his hips. Cecil's bacon squeaked in the pan. John poured out goat's milk for the children.

'A society founded on blood,' he remarked.

'What?'

'Calves killed and cows kept in unnatural lactation.'

'Oh, yes.'

How to provide non-animal protein for the children? He had written for advice to the Vegan Society, but had apparently addressed it wrongly. To his horror, it lay on his plate with 'I suppose this is your idea of a joke!' scrawled across it in his father's writing.

'Someone at the door, Daddy.'

Aaron came in with a fuzz of drizzle on his collar.

'I hope I'm not interrupting your breakfast. I'm afraid I've come too early.' He looked at John.

'Yes,' said Marguerite savagely, it could have been the

hissing of an egg. She started clattering the dishes off the table into the sink.

'But Mummy, we haven't had breakfast yet.'

'Oh.' She put them back, a flame of anger licking each cheekbone.

'May I see the patient?'

The goat was led in and laid her gentle doric face on his knee.

'Ah, yes. I'll give you some ointment. Can you call round for it later this morning, at about eleven, say?'

'Yes.'

'Good, I'll see myself out.'

He ran a hand over Ivan's dense curls.

Marguerite was angry with herself for having asked him to come, angry with her family for appearing so unkempt, angry with herself for minding.

'How about sliding a razor over that muzzle,' she asked, rubbing the back of her hand under John's chin.

'I'm not trying to impress anyone,' he replied.

'Least of all me, I suppose.'

A spiral of frying bacon scent drifted up the stairs and under Cecil's door. He sank back in the dust of the room. 'Oh,' he thought, 'if only I could be satisfied with a frugal egg and not long for more and more marmalade and a caravan of toast.'

John volunteered to do the shopping.

'I'll take you to the park when I get back,' he told the children.

'I'm going to the shops. Can I get you anything, Cecil?'

'I don't think so, thanks.'

Outside Cecil's door he gnashed his teeth and grazed his knuckles punching the embossed wallpaper; he had expected Cecil to offer him some money. He plunged his fist into his penniless coat pocket and banged the glass door behind him. In the High Road he saw a strange familiar figure making chopping motions at her hand; at first he thought she was parodying Mick's accident but as he neared Elizabeth he realized she was quite unaware of him, and they passed without speaking. She was preoccupied with the question of whether it was worth a serious accident to her hand to avoid cooking and sharing Christmas dinner with an old roadsweeper. If so, how to let him know? He was bound to trundle up bearing a clumsily gaily wrapped gift, which he could ill afford from his poor wages. Would a bandaged paw then suffice to turn him away? The idea of closing the curtains, locking the door and spending Christmas lying on the floor was of course unthinkable; but not quite as unthinkable as it had been yesterday. Suddenly it occurred to her that Gibby had not said anything about her Christmas plans. The thought of the three of them round the festal bird drove her over the edge into the gutter, where only the superb steering of a pantechnicon driver saved her problem from being solved for ever.

A cortège passed.

> Groom was there none to see
> The mourners followed after.

John stopped himself and reflected, as he stood in the warm supermarket, on the perils of a retentive memory. Every time a funeral passed, and this was often, because there were two vast cemeteries in the vicinity, he said those lines. His mind was a rest home for old, worn out, forgotten things: hoary advertising jingles from commercial television's dawn broke into their old sprightly dances on its lawns; an old projector showed silent reels of childhood scenes accompanied by high density crooning from a bakelite wireless (there was even a weighty black battery model on some shelf); one window was blacked out, the bathroom was crammed with sinks and cisterns each with its maker's name in unfading letters. The inmates put on their own shows; books shouted facts, words laughed, gramophones spouted music, clothes danced and rustled and shook, faces giggled and gabbled, the plumbing gurgled, the foundations trembled, the whole house shook and shook and shook.

John leaned against the wire basket; someone was staring at him. He knew time had passed but not whether a second or a century, his head throbbed as if in the aftermath of a Bacchanalia. He went out into the air and let the wind mould his head and calm it. Another funeral was traversing the zebra crossing. He dreaded the day when Emily should ask the purpose of those flowery cars. 'Why does it hurt the heart to think,' he began. The children knew about death but not burial, and Ivan sometimes said at bedtime, 'I'll be sad when you die.' His parents, in tones varying from reasonable to jocular, replied: 'But I'm not going to die for years and years until I'm very old, and you'll be grown up with children of your own by then.'

'But I'll be sad when you die.' The lower lip trembled. Having once committed himself to dying, he could not now deny it.

Meanwhile John froze in front of a baker's window, watching the ephemeral confections intimating futility.

The breakfast dishes were spangled with tiny bubbles on the draining-board, the floor washed, beds made, children dressed and occupied, Cecil was singing in contraposition to the radio, and two clouds parted and sun poured through to illuminate these facts. Marguerite stood entranced. A phrase flickered in letters of sun on the wall. Positive thinking. Positive thinking — the solution had bubbled up from her brain to lighten her life. She could run the house, look after the children, be nice to Cecil, see Aaron and John — the letters dimmed, well, positive thinking would show her the way.

The phone rang.

'I'll get it.'

'Elizabeth.' Positive thinking made her repeat the name in glowing tones.

'Elizabeth!'

'Yes, it is me.' Elizabeth sounded surprised at the realization that she and her sister-in-law were such friends.

'How are the children? I've been meaning to ring for ages, but I've been so busy with the end of term and everything.'

'Yes.'

'A friend of mine's having a party tonight. It's Eric Turle. I think you've met him. He wondered if you and John would like to come.'

As Elizabeth spoke an escape route began forming in Marguerite's head.

'I'm sure we'd love to. The thing is I'll have to see if Cecil can babysit. Where is it?'

Elizabeth gave her the address.

'I do hope you can make it. It would be super to see you both.'

'Yes, look forward to seeing you later then. Thanks for ringing.'

An implosion of giggles in the receiver puzzled

Marguerite as she put it down; she wasn't to know that Gibby, standing behind Elizabeth in the phone box and making faces in the mirror, had been overcome by mirth and had laughed the directory off the shelf and on to Elizabeth's foot.

She hung her black velvet trousers in the bathroom so that they would be groomed by steam from Cecil's bath and took a variegated silk shirt from an unpacked suitcase in the bedroom. Hitherto she had felt too sombre to wear it.

Cecil was thrilled to be asked to babysit. He began making plans at once.

'If they wake I'll make them a cup of chocolate and read them a story, and if they –'

'But Cecil, they hardly ever wake and they don't like –'

'Be prepared.'

Marguerite was very pleased to be going out. She had felt they were losing face with Cecil and this added an aura of shame to their gloom.

She looked up from the book she was reading to the children to see John standing there with an empty wire supermarket basket.

'What's that? Where's the shopping?'

He stared down at it, his knuckles tightened to white bone on the handle.

'I … I … I must have picked it up instead of the full one – I suppose I'd better go back –'

'No. No, you sit down, you look exhausted. I'll go. Do you feel all right?'

She was putting them on the right footing so that he would agree to go to the party, and would refuse to pronounce him ill, but when she put her hand on his forehead and felt the dry moderate skin she was overcome by uxoriousness and her hand strayed up to his damp springy hair like heather in the mist.

'Guess what! I know you'll be pleased. Elizabeth rang, and she's asked us to a party.'

John wanted to hurl the wire basket through the window and rush upstairs and into bed and pull the blankets over his head, never to emerge.

'A party? When?'

'Tonight. It's at someone called Derek Turtles.'

'Eric Turle. Not that snide.'

'Elizabeth sounded very keen to see you.'

'Let her come round here then. She knows where I am.'

'She's been very busy.'

'Always so damn self-important. Even as a child she always had some stamp collection or homework cluttering up the table, so much more important than my concerns that I had to study on the floor.'

'I'll go and collect that shopping. Goodbye, children, I won't be long.'

'All right then, we'll go.'

John almost spat the concession as she put on her coat to confront the bewildered supermarket staff.

A mild wet wind blew down the road to meet her, lifting her hair and spirits. Pigeons flew in the achromatic sky. She turned left instead of right.

Aaron answered the door in a white overall.

'What a lovely surprise.'

'I may be able to see you tonight. Will you be in?'

'Of course. I have been in every night for the last two weeks. I'm not reproaching you. I'd wait a lifetime to see you for twenty minutes.' His lips seemed slightly meaty in his unshaven face.

I'm getting as bad as John, she thought. 'Thank you. You see we're going to a party and I may be able to slip out for a bit. Anyway I'll try. I must go now.'

'Just a moment, I've got something for you.'

He went in and came back with a long flat silver box of chocolates.

'They're beautiful – but –'

'But what?'

'Oh nothing. Thank you very much. Do you know the time?'

'It's five to one.'

'Oh no!'

'Why? What's wrong?'

'I was supposed to be going shopping, I won't have time now.'

'There's a shop up the road.'

'But I haven't any money,' she almost shouted.

'That's easily solved.'

He put his hand under his overall and drew out a five-pound note.

There was much to be said in his favour.

'Remember my offer.' His words caught at her flying hair.

'Offer?'

'Come back a minute.' He whispered darkly in her ear.

'I'll give you anything you like if you'll spend the night with me!'

'A hundred pounds?'

'Certainly.'

She freed herself from his treacly gaze and ran down the road to the shop where she bought lavishly and filled two carrier bags.

If anyone was sufficiently interested they could amass

such a lot of evidence against me. 'Hallo, everyone. I'm back.'

'Did you get it?' John's voice faltered.

'Yes. They'd already put your stuff away, so they let me pick some more.'

John dared to raise his eyes from *Exchange and Mart*, and gasped.

'All that?'

'Just goes to show that I'm a better shopper than you.'

John knew a miracle had happened and that it was wiser to accept it gratefully without asking why or how.

Marguerite unpacked the bags except for the chocolates, which she concealed in a folded carrier bag and carried upstairs. She knelt on the bedroom floor, and pushed the carrier bag into the dust under the bed, while her mind was compiling lists of Christmas presents that a hundred pounds would buy, crossing them out as impossible, and immediately starting again.

Chapter Sixteen

'Mum, I realize that you're not speaking to me but—'

'Did you say something, Gay?'

'No. Did you?'

'No. Funny, I thought I didn't hear something then.'

'I didn't hear it too.'

'Mum, I'm sorry about the letter.'

'Very cold for the time of year, don't you think?'

'Oh definitely.'

'It would be to your advantage to tell me about the job.' Joy tried not to cry.

' 'Orrible pong in here, can you notice it?'

'Seems to be coming from that direction.'

'If there is, it's your fault,' screamed Joy. 'You never even provided me with the basic essentials of cleanliness.'

'So now I'm dirty, am I?'

'Yes, you're filthy, you never wash. No wonder my dad couldn't stand you. He couldn't stand the smell.'

'Right! You wait, my girl, you just wait.'

Mrs Pickering began tearing off her plimsolls and advanced, one in each hand. Joy dodged her mother, who tripped on the flex of the electric fire and crashed down on to the bed.

'Listen, you thick old witch, if you let me get that job, I'll be able to give you some money, won't I?'

'Hit her, Gay. Go on, land her one!' Mrs Pickering's feet were entangled in washing on the bed.

Joy rushed at Gay, caught her fists and banged them together and held them above her sister's head. A cry broke from their mother's lips.

'Oh my Gawd, she's only broken the bleeding fire.'

Joy dropped Gay's hands. They all stared at the vapour of blue smoke drifting from the torn flex's bared veins.

'You broke it.'

'Your fault though, weren't it,' snapped Gay. 'Now we haven't even got a fire,' she began to wail.

'You better get that job to pay for a new one! You get down to the slaughterhouse in North Pole Road nine o'clock sharp tomorrow, and don't you be late.'

'Slaughterhouse! I'm not going there. You can't make me slaughter animals.'

'I suppose you'd rather Gay and myself froze to death.'

'But I haven't any money. I haven't any clothes!'

But not another word could she milk from their cracked lips. They took off their cardigans, Gay her shoes, and climbed into bed.

Insulated by black rage, Joy burned beneath the blanket, which had also turned black, for two hours. She opened her eyes on piecemeal snowlight through the wasted wool and poked her feet out on to the frozen floor and into her icy shoes. Her mother's old black harridan purse lay on the table; Joy took from it the key on its knotty string, put on her coat and went downstairs. As she pulled the launderette door to behind her, her foot sent a milk bottle chiming across the pavement. She retrieved it from the gutter and was going to replace it, but kept it in her hand – a glass club.

'Where are you going?' A boy of about her own age,

abroad in the night for reasons of his own, fell into step beside her. She recognized something within him and let him walk with her.

'I'm going to kill someone.'

'Where does he live?'

'Not very far.'

The travelling companions continued on their way.

'A lot of people in this road seem to have cars. Two-car families, what do you bet?'

Joy nodded silently.

'No, look, that house is all lit up. Must be a party.'

'Oh no!'

'That the house then?'

'Looks like it.'

'What now?'

'You don't have to wait.'

'I don't mind.'

They went into the front garden and crouched among leaves sticky with snow beside the garage. The curtains had been pulled back so that the guests could watch the snow; music fell with the flakes.

'Ring the bell and run back quickly,' said Joy.

Her acolyte obeyed. The door was flung open. The opener must have been right behind it. Gibby stood puzzled on the step. Joy heard Miriam Turle's voice float out of the open door,

'But I've hardly danced a step all night,' and Eric's odious voice answered in heartfelt tones, 'I know!'

And he hopped in the hall rubbing his foot as the door swung to and hid him from the watchers in the garden.

'That's him.'

'He looks a right bastard.'

'He is. Are you sure you want to wait?'

'I don't mind.'

Joy, suddenly realizing that she was alone with and accepted by a boy, became anxious for his comfort.

'There's a stone here you can sit on.'

'It's all right.'

Joy rang the bell and darted back.

'Ee-ric Tu-urle! Ee-ric Tu-urle!'

Turle peeped round the door.

'Come out here, Turle!'

'Who is it? Where are you?'

'Co-ome ou-out, Ee-ric Turle. Your ti-time is up. Your so-oul is required!'

She was gratified by his cowardice.

'We've come to kill you!'

'Who are you? Stay where you are!'

'Miriam,' he croaked.

Two spectral assassins stepped out of the shadows; one raised a phantasmal arm to strike him. Gibbering, Turle stepped back grabbing the letterbox. His heart hurting, pleading, shielding his face, petrified as the lycanthropic bloody-bones came inexorably towards him, a cloud of fetid breath —

'Joy Pickering! I thought I told you never to come back here.'

Turle crumpled in a whimpering heap on Miriam's feet.

Joy's companion rolled a swift wet snowball and flung it, and Miriam, anchored by her husband to the step, received the full splat smack in the face.

Joy and her friend fled. 'Whatever happens,' she gasped, 'I'll always love you for that snowball.'

She realized they were holding hands.

'Joy! Joy!'

Elizabeth overtook them, exuding liquor and sincerity.

'Joy, what made you do it?'

'This lady bothering you, darlin'?'

'Yes, she is.'

'You heard what she said. Get lost.'

'Joy, you will try hard to get that job, for my sake? Or I shall feel so guilty for letting you leave school without more protest. You could have had a fine G.C.E. result.'

'Elizabeth!'

John had followed her from the house.

'I wouldn't work in a slaughterhouse if they paid me,' Joy shouted at her. The desperadoes increased their pace and were gone.

'Oh John, that's the girl I was trying to help. It seems she's turning down a perfectly good job at the abattoir. It's just no use trying to help some people!'

Back in the house Eric seized Elizabeth, whirled her into a dance, nuzzling the melting snowflakes from her hair. John stood by the piano and thought of his father sitting straight-backed at the upright piano, thundering out the "Internationale", with Elizabeth's sweet voice and John's which ambled over the keyboard, hitting here a black note, there a white, on either side of him. Or even occasionally "Cwm Rhondda", that trap for the voice unsure whether it is contralto, tenor or soprano. He could see the snow flattening the corrugated iron roof of the transport café between Foots Cray and Sidcup or nowhere that his parents had taken when he was seven.

A tin sign that flapped and rattled in the bleak winds blowing off the ploughed fields before and behind; men stepping out of the great lorries that rolled over the cinder forecourt; his father's uneasy mateyness; the chicken-run full of disused rabbit hutches, tyres, and a solid paper sack of cement; yesterday's dry sandwiches fried for breakfast; the Party party where everyone sang, 'We'll make Sir Winston Churchill smoke a Woodbine every day, When the Red Revolution comes'.

John felt an intense sadness. He drank down a glass of whisky he found on the piano and it decided him that the time had come to tell Marguerite about his lost job.

He moved through the party with his bad news like a vulture on his shoulder.

'Not talking to anyone, John?' Miriam Turle was barring his way.

'There doesn't seem to be anyone of my sort here.'

'And what sort is that?'

'The jobless, G.C.E.-less genius.'

'Ah, I don't think Tim here's got any.'

'Do you mind? I've got woodwork.' Tim flounced off.

'Actually I'm looking for my wife.'

'Oh, Marguerite asked me to tell you she had a headache and she's slipped off home. She didn't want to spoil the party for you. So come and have a dance with me. I am your hostess,' she added.

'Did you know I'd been offered the Literary Editorship of *Eclogue*?' Eric asked Elizabeth.

'Really? That's super! Congratulations.'

'Yes, the former editor just collapsed and died at his desk. Rather nice to go in harness, don't you think?'

Elizabeth doubted if she'd care to expire into the custard while on dinner duty, but smiled enthusiastically.

'What's your sister-in-law like?' he asked, secretly peeved because she had left without dancing with him.

'Very nice—a bit shallow though, I think. I once heard her say that insulating tape is the most depressing thing in the world.'

*

Marguerite reached past Aaron's sleeping head for his watch, and moved the hands to half past four.

'Aaron, wake up! It's half past four. You owe me a hundred pounds.'

He sat up and the sheet fell back from the pretty whorls and shells of hair on his chest, and with eyes still closed he patted about the floor for his trousers and handed her a wad of notes.

'Merry Christmas, darling.'

'Oh Aaron. Ten ten-pound notes, how distinguished!'

'We must get you home. I'd better not drive you. I'll ring for a taxi.'

He took her in his arms and drew her to his chest, his fingers slid over her old silver satin slip, she kissed his massive head.

'I love your head, it's so huge.' She knocked with her knuckles on bone.

'What a memento mori a head is, isn't it?'

'I'll get that taxi.'

As the taxi accelerated she knew she would have to make it turn. She pulled back the glass partition.

'Please go back, I've forgotten something.'

Aaron looked as if he had been woken again.

'Aaron, I tricked you. It isn't half past four, and I can't possibly take your money.'

'I know. But you must take your Christmas present.'

'I can't, it isn't right. I should never have suggested it. I can't see you any more either.'

'What are you saying? Of course you can.'

'No. I realized what my priorities are when you gave me the money. I wanted it for presents for the children. It's humiliating for you.'

'And John?'

'And John.'

'But there's no need to stop seeing me. You need me. Life's so boring without you. Aren't you bored?'

She laughed. She wanted to be buried in him.

'Yes, I have to admit it is a bit boring.'

'I get so bored!'

'But when it's a choice between boredom and panic, there's a lot to be said for boredom!'

'There's a lot to be said for panic. When I leave you I'm in such a state of euphoria I'm always losing things. Last time I drove the wrong way down a one-way street.'

'You can't fit an extra piece into a jigsaw.'

The taxi driver honked.

'I can't bear to think of you going specially to the bank for this, please take it back.'

'If you don't take it I'll donate it to vivisection.' He put it back in her bag and snapped it shut.

'Enjoy spending it. I hope you and the children have a happier Christmas than I. Goodbye, Marguerite. I know we'll meet again, if only when I come to cut my throat on your doorstep.'

'Goodbye, Aaron.'

Goodbye champagne, taxis, illicit day turned to night.

'Don't cry.'

'I'm not,' as something splashed on her lip.

At home she discharged Cecil from his watch. The children hadn't woken; Cecil went to bed. Marguerite put her hand in her bag and felt the money, but she couldn't look at it yet. She didn't want to go to bed, her eye fell on a copy of *Dalton's Weekly* and she sat at the kitchen table and began reading the front page.

A fingernail chirruped on the back door. Thinking it was Doris's horn Marguerite opened the door and Doris jumped up from beneath the table and rushed out, and Aaron's head looked in.

'Are you alone?'

'Yes.'

He came in.

'Is John back?'

'No.'

'Lock the front door, and I'll have time to nip out the back if he gets back. He won't be back before four.'

'How do you know? You always assume that people will act to suit you —' she began but shrugged and went to lock the door. Cecil's snores cut swathes of night air.

'You can't do without me, you know.'

He put a Christmas paper bag on the table and took out a bottle of champagne. Marguerite silently fetched two glasses.

'I think I'll just pop this into the fridge for a minute,' he said, as if endless night would unroll like a starry carpet before them.

'Please just open it.'

He did and lit two cigarettes.

'Here's to us.'

She drank silently.

The door glided open. Marguerite sat transfixed. Emily stood smiling in the doorway, smiling at the audible gust of relief.

'Emily. What on earth are you doing here?'

Aaron looked at Marguerite and saw, instead of the expected reflection of his horror, a great smile on her face.

'I've come for two Garibaldi biscuits.'

And the inconvenient child was larded with kisses for her temerity, the gilt-and-red tin was brought forth and she was fêted with biscuits and at last Aaron, having failed utterly to notice the sweetness of her pyjamas, her eyes describing incredible arcs, saw her gathered up with more tenderness than he would ever get. While they disappeared among murmurs of toothbrushes, and promises of water, he quietly poured the champagne down the sink, picked up the cork from the floor and replaced it and the bottle in the festive bag whence they came, emptied in the cigarette butts from the ashtray, gathered up gold flakes of foil and shook them all in a melancholy cocktail as he quietly closed the front door behind him.

'He's a dead loss at a party.' John heard a voice behind his back.

'Who is he?'

'Nobody.'

'I thought so.'

The inhabitants of his memory had hauled out the fading scenery and were staging a show. A coachload of militant gourmets rolled up in the car park outside the transport café; they sampled the tea and coffee, broke the bread, sniffed the ketchup, left the chips dying stranded in pools of fat on their plates, rolled the fruitcake into balls and pelted each other, while his mother screamed and his father ran about threatening and pleading in his apron. They finally began breaking up chairs and twisting the plastic heads of flowers. They rumbled away before the police arrived, but his mother never recovered from the insult to her cooking. In court their counsel pleaded mitigating circumstances and their fines were halved; the publicity didn't do the place much good. Fewer lorries seemed to stop now, support for the Party dwindled and died, and John's father was left with only the television to argue with. His mother kept a damp cloth handy on the arm of her viewing chair to wipe off the missiles he hurled at the screen.

They were woken by the telephone. Mrs Wood clung to her husband in the big bed.

'Don't go!'

'It might be important.'

He didn't want to go either, but the phone shrilled on, skewering him out of bed.

'Hallo. Hallo. Who is it?'

'Hallo, Dad.'

'John. Have you any idea of the time.'

'No.'

John's voice came faintly through a blur of voices and music.

'Would you and Mum come up here to Cecil's for Christmas? We all want you to.'

'Yes. Good night! Cecil's already invited us.'

'Dad, just a minute. There's something I've always wanted to ask you, but didn't dare. Who won the Spanish Civil War?'

'Do you realize it's four months since your mother heard from you? I'll see you at Christmas.'

He hung up.

Now John's school song was pealing through the smoke to break his heart and when he turned he saw Gibby floating past in a school hat. She had been rifling a cupboard and in her convulsions failed to realize that nobody shared her glee.

'Come on, Elizabeth, let's give them a verse of the old school song.' She dragged Elizabeth on to a chair and they swayed together, shouting, snorting and giggling the old words and the chorus. Gibby's voice broke; she couldn't go on, but Elizabeth heard her own voice soaring on and still had sufficient awareness to be dimly thankful that every dancer was steadfastly ignoring them.

Gibby jumped down.

'Damn. I didn't expect it to take me like that.'

She rushed into the kitchen, tore off the hat and flung it; it skimmed the air and landed on the Aga. A row of Christmas cards hung on a tinsel line across the mantelpiece. Before she knew it she was back in the party with someone sloshing something red into her glass.

'Have some plonk.'

'I won't say no,' reflecting that she never did.

'Elizabeth, there's something I want to discuss with you.'

'Not a reminiscence?'

'No. I phoned home this morning and Mother said she and Dad are going to the Costa Brava for Christmas.'

'Super.'

'Which leaves little old me at a bit of a loose end.'

'Hmm, I suppose it does.'

A face loomed between them but caught in the intensity of the two girls faded away.

'What are you going to do?'

'I'll think of something, I suppose. Don't worry about me. I'll be all right.'

Gibby squared her shoulders pluckily and pushed her way through the crowd, but her head was bowed.

'Gibby! Please spend Christmas with me. I was assuming you would anyway. It won't be the same without you.'

She turned, a radiant tear trembling on her nose, and

squeezed Elizabeth's hand until her best friend had to beg for mercy. Oh God. Gibby and the old roadsweeper. Oh God.

'This calls for a celebration! Where's that plonk? Do you remember when we used to do the conga through the classrooms at the end of term? Come on! Where's that gloomy brother of yours. I'll soon liven him up!'

John heard and fled.

'You've never liked me, have you?' called Gibby bitterly after him.

He collided with Eric in the doorway as he dashed out.

'What a rude person! That's the last time I ask them to a party!' Gibby chugged on and rounded up enough support for a puny conga which burst at its first collision and its links scattered never to re-form. Gibby had discovered she could balance a tray of glasses and peanuts on her head. Well, almost.

It was ten to five; Miriam was asleep fully dressed on the bed; the guests had all gone except the lady who had asked to see some of Eric's poems and had been regretting it for the last two hours. In the kitchen the school hat had been reduced to a scorched pancake and the Christmas cards were nicely browned and curling up at the edges.

At eight o'clock, the first riser, Marguerite crept out of bed leaving John asleep. She had been disturbed in the early hours by the ominous rattle of the Andrews tin. In the cold sitting-room she sat at Cecil's desk and took his pen and a sheet of paper, the morning light illuminating the down on her arms like the hairs on the geranium stems; the black earthy cat's-paw smell engulfing her as she wrote.

Wednesday   *Rhododendrons*
                                              Isle of Wight

My Dears,

Daddy and I want you to have this. Buy something
really nice for yourselves and the children.

I'm sorry we shan't be seeing you at Christmas —

The letterbox flapped. She gathered up her letter and
ran, a knocking in the ribs, bare knees knocking to the
hall. There was one letter, addressed to her. Back in the
sitting-room she opened it and two five-pound notes fell
to the carpet. It read:

Wednesday   *Rhododendrons*
                                              Isle of Wight

My Dears,

Daddy and I want you to have this. Buy something
for yourselves and the children. I'm sorry we shan't
be seeing you this Christmas but —

Marguerite hurriedly folded the notes into the envelope. She felt unaccountably guilty, as if she had
spurned her mother's present. She destroyed her own
letter, and put five of the ten-pound notes into her
mother's envelope. The rest of the money she hid in an
old bag at the bottom of the wardrobe and went down
to make the children's breakfast. She took John's up on
a tray and propped her mother's letter against his boiled
egg.

He came whooping down the stairs, embraced
Marguerite, waltzed with the goat, kissed the children,
took a great slurp of porridge from the pot and skipped
out again with burning mouth.

Meanwhile Eric Turle stood in the remains of his blackened kitchen; the window was shrouded in soot, the table charred, the walls festooned with trails of smoke, the black Christmas tree topiarized by flame, and sooty puddles everywhere. The telephone rang.

'Hallo, Eric?' a small uncertain voice was heard. 'This is Gibby. Thank you for a lovely party.'

Marguerite took the children, and all the money, Christmas shopping, they bought John a pair of cord Levis (hopeful of leg length), a shirt and a sweater, a cardigan and tie for Cecil, presents for all the parents, cards, stamps, decorations, green and gold corduroy trousers for the children, a vegetarian Christmas pudding to complement Cecil's suety cannonball, icing sugar, nuts, tangerines. Marguerite knew that the buying had to stop this side of credibility and bought a last flamboyant box of crackers.

John bruised his knuckles on Mick's broken door-knocker. Mick poked out his stubble head.

'What do you want now? Come back for another dose, have you? Hang on, I'll call me mate.'

'I've heard of a job in your line of business. If you're interested.'

'I'm interested.'

'There's a job going at the slaughterhouse. Only you'll have to get down there right away.'

'Thanks, mate.'

Mick stepped out on to the balcony and revealed himself in striped pyjamas, and shook John warmly with both hands, at which John dared not look.

'Thanks.'

'Only too pleased to help.'

'Perhaps I can shove some your way. You never know.'

'No thanks. I don't eat meat.'

'What are you having for Christmas then?'

'Oh, er—nuts and, er, bolts, that sort of thing—'

'Well, ta, anyway. I won't forget you.'

'Please do.'

John ran down the steps, sweating hot with relief at having made some amends.

In the afternoon Cecil took the children to the park while Marguerite and John went shopping for their presents; a doll's pram for Emily, and a chubby red rigid plastic pedal-car for Ivan that honked mysteriously in the wardrobe in the middle of the night.

Marguerite woke to find Doris on her knees with her head under the bed devouring whole the silver box of chocolates. 'A just penance,' she thought, and went back to sleep.

The last double doors of the Calendar opened to reveal the crib, Mary, Joseph, Jesus and an adoring donkey.

Chapter Seventeen

'It's no good. It just won't cook with the oven door half open.'

'Here, give it to me.'

Gibby sawed the turkey in two and put one half on each shelf of the oven.

'He's here. For goodness sake go and get dressed, Gib.'

Gibby closed the bedroom door as the bell rang. Elizabeth hastily Sellotaped the ends of the parcel of aftershave. He hadn't shaved.

'A kiss under the mistletoe.' He lunged for her under the naked lampshade. His breath stank of spirits.

'Stop it, you've been drinking!' He grabbed her to his filthy overcoat and stuck his face like a sea urchin on to hers.

'Get off, you filthy old man! Get out!'

He stared at her and as he jerked her head back she knew she was looking into Joy Pickering's eyes.

'Get out, get out. You stink.'

'What you ask me round for then?'

He grabbed a wooden spoon from the table and bent her forward and began to hit her.

'Ow! Ooh! Stop!' she yelled.

'That'll learn you,' he gave her a final blow and pushed her away. She slid to the floor.

'Women!' he exclaimed as he took the bottle of sherry from the draining-board, and slammed the door.

Gibby was laughing from the bedroom door.

'Well, you have to see the funny side,' she gasped.

Elizabeth leapt at her with a roar and slapped her face, then switched off the oven, grabbed her coat and a bagful of presents and galloped up the road. Gibby pulled her own coat on and followed her, unencumbered by presents. Still smarting, the two friends arrived simultaneously at Cecil's door.

'Come in. Come and join the party.'

Elizabeth saw a vague elderly couple perched on two chairs pushed against the wall; in a moment their contours reassembled into those of her parents.

She rushed guiltily through tinsel trip-wires and tissue briars, a goat's horn poked through a shower of gold foil grazing her leg, and embraced them, her first true impression already blurred with familiarity. It seemed too much to believe that Gibby could contrive to step over the goat's rising head and be pitched at the feet of Elizabeth's parents, but she did, reinforcing their opinion of her. She looked up at the laughing children and saw that they were wearing new clothes. Christmas for them at least was all it should be. Father Christmas, who, perhaps in revenge for the gnawed mince pies and sherry dregs on her mantelpiece, had long since ignored little Gibby's chimney, had visited last night. But Gibby had once heard sleigh bells and believed.

'Did Santa Claus come last night?' she stooped and asked.

'Yes! He brought us lots of lovely things and we left him a mince pie.'

'Aah,' said Gibby, as if in pain, and snatched a dangling stocking and turned it inside out, as if there might be a message for her in the toe.

Cecil's brocade waistcoat came bobbing in like a chinese lantern.

'Lunch is just ready. John, two extra chairs. Ladies and gentlemen, pray be seated!'

John's father lifted Emily, chair and all, so that he could sit next to his son, while his mother placed herself between her grandchildren and tucked a holly-bordered napkin into each of their necks.

'John,' said his father, rolling a melancholy eye over the mound of cold sprouts, 'I thought you might be interested to know that I ran into old Wally Walterson last week.'

'Oh yes?'

He remembered wet fellow-travelling pamphleteering bookseller Wally, who loved to wind a finger through the curls at John's nape, pulling up on the street corner, sheaf of unsold papers in his arm, shirt open revealing ravelling silver steel wool on his chest.

'Yes. Poor fellow had a stroke, you know.'

'Oh dear.'

'Yes. He's my age, you know.'

'Is he?'

'Yes. But don't keep interrupting, John, let me get to the point … '

Gibby had found a giant cracker and thrust the free end in John's mother's face. It exploded right behind Ivan's head. He jumped.

'You might have broken the glass in my eyes,' he said indignantly. Emily rushed to put her arm round his shoulders and glared round the table.

'Sit down everyone, please,' begged Marguerite.

Cecil raised his glass.

'The point is, John,' said his father quickly, 'He can't cope with the business any more — his daughter's sold out to the bourgeoisie — he needs someone younger, with ideas, who can reorganize the whole stock, inject new life into the place … '

Cecil lowered his glass.

'Ahem. May I have your attention please?' A touch of rattiness crept into his tone.

'The point is, John, I recommended you, as a man of ideas, and he's willing to give you a chance. It'll mean hard work of course … '

'I shan't mind that,' said John, his eyes bright with purpose as well as Cecil's nutty sherry. He became aware that all eyes looked kindly on him and hid his face in his plate from the unexpected sunshine.

Cecil raised his glass.

'John promised to make this the best Christmas we've ever had and it looks as if he's going to succeed. Merry Christmas, everyone!'

'There's a couple of rooms above the shop,' Mr Wood's voice was heard.

John and Marguerite's eyes met through a glaze of tears.

'Merry Christmas! Merry Christmas! Merry Christmas!'

And there we leave them, carousing on a sandbank in time, music and laughter, forks and glasses drowning the sound of tomorrow's tide.